PLUNDER TRAIL
Robert E. Trevathan

Dan Yeager's ankle was broken, his uncle was dead, and their wagon was ruined. All in all, Dan didn't have one chance in a million of catching up with Jink Barrett and the other outlaws who had stolen his uncle's barrel containing forty-eight sets of flatware and other silver items that were to be delivered at Fort Gibson. Even if Dan miraculously managed to catch up with the Barrett gang, he'd never be able to get back the stolen goods.

So why try? Because whether his ankle was broken or not — whether he had a realistic chance or not — Dan Yeager was one very determined young man. And somehow he was going to have the last laugh!

PLUNDER TRAIL

Robert E. Trevathan

AVALON BOOKS
THOMAS BOUREGY AND COMPANY, INC.
NEW YORK

PRINTED IN THE UNITED STATES OF AMERICA
BY HADDON CRAFTSMEN, SCRANTON, PENNSYLVANIA

Plunder Trail

Chapter 1

The three younger members of Jink Barrett's gang patiently sat their mounts, waiting for the silvermith's wagon to come into view again. Sixty-year-old Seep Jessup, the fourth member of Barrett's outfit, half dozed on the seat of the gang's plunder wagon in the woods forty yards behind the three gunmen.

Jessup wasn't expected to take part in the actual holdups even though, despite his age, he was competent with any weapon he could get his hands on. It was understood that his job was just to cook for the others and to tend to the four fast Spanish mules that pulled the plunder wagon.

It was midafternoon and getting very warm under the Texas sun. Jink Barrett pushed back his hat with the huge bear's claw buckle at the front.

"What do you say, Fluke?" Jink asked as the wagon with the silver returned to their

1

line of vision. "Sid Yeager and his nephew killed your only brother—and he was my cousin, too—when we tried to pull that job at their silver shop in San Antonio. You can keep teasing them along, taking potshots at their cookfire every night—or we can end matters right now."

Fluke-Eye slouched sideways on his dun. His left eye moved around wildly—not like his normal right eye—and it gave him an odd look. He didn't let it bother him, though, because he was still a first-class shot. That was the important thing.

Fluke nodded now, saying, "Fun time is over for them, Cousin. Let's nail both of 'em."

"You're set then?"

Fluke-Eye's hand strayed from the butt of his revolver and patted the stock of the Sharps carbine in his saddle boot. "That Uncle Sid is mine, so you others take care of Danny boy."

Barrett twisted in his saddle and addressed the third man. "Rim, need I ask you?"

Rim Alum, a big man with a double-barreled shotgun and reddish whiskers, puffed on a fat cigar stub. "No decision to make here, Jink. I haven't been with you for long, but you an' Fluke-Eye have that score to even up—an' there they go rolling along. They've got a tarp snugged down over their stuff—and we know they're carrying silver. Let's send 'em down the ravine! I don't think anything will go wrong. But just in case, we all know where our meeting place is up the road. So let's go!"

Jink Barrett rubbed his thick beard, then unholstered his revolver. "Too bad for them—but Dan Yeager should have shoved their cash box beneath that counter to his uncle instead of that derringer. That wasn't being cooperative at all."

Seconds later Fluke-Eye leveled his carbine, took quick aim, and squeezed the trigger. Other shots rapidly followed, shattering the afternoon.

Sid Yeager was hit dead center in the heart, and one of his two white mules was shot in the chest. The badly wounded animal stumbled, while the wagon bounced over some ruts.

Young Dan Yeager never knew it, but one of those ruts saved his life. For the bullet aimed at him only clipped his shirt collar.

Another shot creased the second mule just below the head, making that animal stumble, too.

As the wagon lurched toward a fallen log,

Dan glanced over his shoulder and had a quick look at the three gunmen, noting particularly the bearded rider in the middle with the familiar bear's claw buckle on his hatband. Dan knew they were the same men who'd tried to rob him and his uncle in the silver shop a month ago. Ever since then he'd thought of the leader as the Bear Claw Man, and he knew the one with the wild expression in his left eye was called Fluke.

That whole robbery fiasco hadn't taken a minute. Uncle Sid had shot one of the holdup men with the derringer, and his cohorts had pulled the gunman out of the shop without stealing anything.

Belatedly, Dan tried to grab the reins from his dead uncle's hands, but it was hopeless. Hitting the fallen log, the wagon lost a wheel and skittered off the road toward the brush-covered ravine below.

Additional shots rang out as Dan was thrown far from the shattered wagon, which was now slamming into some boulders by the creek in the middle of the ravine. As darkness swirled around him, he vaguely thought his Uncle Sid simply hadn't been destined to complete the trip to Fort Gibson to deliver the promised forty-eight sets of silverware and the other finely made items.

Dan was completely unconscious as the Jink Barrett gang rushed down the ravine and located the barrel with the valuables. They checked Sid Yeager—who'd been thrown a fair distance from the wagon—to make sure he was dead. Next they looked in vain for his nephew. Then, when Rim Alum happened to spot Dan's hat floating in the creek, they assumed if a bullet hadn't finished him off, a lungful of water had.

So the Barrett outfit called off the search, hauled up the barrel, and returned to their plunder wagon.

Chapter 2

It was a while before a tiny pocket in Dan's mind began coming back to life. Now he was faintly aware of considerable activity above the ravine where he lay in a hollow spot near the creek, concealed by dense shrubs. There was a rumbling, horn-clacking sound of a small herd of cattle passing by, and the unmistakable creaking noise of wagon wheels. He heard a mumble of voices, too.

When he finally roused himself and started to get up, the pain in his right ankle told him he had a bad sprain or perhaps a fracture. He blinked his eyes, realizing that moonlight was bathing the area, coming through the treetops. Reaching about on the ground, he found a dead limb and, breaking off the twigs, he used it to limp toward the shattered pieces of the wagon, looking for his Uncle Sid.

But Dan didn't have any luck.

However, he did find one of the white

7

mules lying partially in the water of the creek. He could see it was Domino, the older one. And he was dead.

Well, maybe Judy, the other mule, was still alive somewhere nearby. Dan continued to move about, looking for his uncle. But he had no luck in the dark.

Meanwhile, the voices above the ravine seemed a little clearer and the wagon wheels weren't moving anymore. That told Dan the group was probably camping nearby for the night.

Hoping the strangers would be friendly, Dan tried to ignore the throbbing pain in his right ankle as he scrambled up and over the edge of the ravine. By the time he came to the road, his head was swimming, his lungs pulling in big gulps of air. Pausing, catching his breath, he saw a campfire a short distance away.

Dan also saw three wagons, two of them seemingly connected in a tandem arrangement underneath a big live oak. Several horses were staked out nibbling grass at the edge of a small clearing along the road.

The campfire glowed near the rear of one of the wagons, something cooking in a pot on a rod above it—and a slight breeze wafted a tantalizing aroma in Dan's direction.

But what claimed the bulk of Dan's attention was the big man who was standing on his head on what appeared to be a flat box of some kind with a hollow in it made to fit his skull. This heavyset individual was wiggling back and forth, adjusting his balance, twisting his legs.

Dan blinked in wonderment, almost forgetting the pain climbing up from his ankle.

The big man suddenly dropped to his feet and picked up a circular piece of material from the box where his head had been. The material looked all shiny and wet in the fire glow, and the man abruptly twisted it in his huge hands, wringing it out on the ground, squeezing with great strength, dribbling water between thick fingers.

Turning toward the single wagon, which had a Dutch door built into the rear, he announced:

"This'll just about do it, Cabe, make me the best rawhide hat you'd ever hope to see anywhere. Take a gander."

An oldster's head poked into view in the opened upper portion of the Dutch door. A brier pipe slanted from one corner of his mouth, a spiral of smoke trickling upward.

"Make sure that hole's plenty big enough for your head, Ester," he advised. "You know how rawhide shrinks."

Ester said, "Don't worry, Cabe. I know what I'm doing when it comes to working with any kind of leather."

All the same, he put the hat back in the flat box—the mold—then whapped and hammered at the piece of leather with his meaty hands as if to make doubly sure he had enough space in the crown of his new hat. "Fresh hide does have a tendency to dry some smaller," Ester allowed.

"True enough," Cabe said. He knocked some ashes from his pipe on the side of his wagon, then ducked inside and began rattling things noisily as he attended to some chore.

Dan took a deep breath. The bantering pair before him seemed amiable enough on the surface, but that didn't show how they might react to some stranger. Still, he needed help. So he started to move toward them.

He had just taken a few steps when he tripped and fell. Dan could not help crying out, for a flash of pain was rolling up his leg.

The man called Ester reacted quickly, his right hand streaking to the butt of a .44 Colt as he sprang into the nearby shadows.

"I need some help," Dan called out, knowing that Ester couldn't see him because of the shrubbery separating them. "No harm intended."

The clattering stopped inside Cabe's wagon, and the oldster appeared at his half-opened doorway. "What is it, Ester? You started talking to yourself again? These long trips do strange things to a man."

"Stand by, Cabe," Ester said cautiously. "Sounds as if we have company." Then, pointing his weapon in Dan's direction, he came forward slowly, saying, "Friend or enemy? Which might you be, huh?"

"Real friendly," Dan said. "But don't ask me to get up with my arms over my head because I don't think I can make it."

"Why, what's the matter?" Ester asked.

"I'm hurt—my ankle."

Ester peered closely at Dan in the moonlight. Dan could not only see the big man's revolver, he also glimpsed a rifle barrel in the upper portion of the Dutch door. So he knew that old Cabe was ready for action, too.

"What's going on, Ester?" Cabe inquired.

"I'm about to find out," the big man murmured, taking another cautious step forward.

"What's your name?" Ester demanded gruffly, silhouetted against the cookfire behind him.

"Dan Frank—"

"Two front names?"

"Dan Frank Yeager."

"What're you doing spying on us?" Ester asked.

"I'm not spying or anything like that."

"Let's see here." Keeping Dan covered, Ester knelt down beside him, his free hand moving over Dan's body rapidly and surely, searching for weapons. Finding a Green River knife at Dan's hip, he deftly removed it from its leather sheath and slipped it into a sheath he evidently had inside his left boot.

"I'll just take this knife for right now if you don't mind—or even if you do, Dan Frank Yeager. So happens I collect good knives, and yours has a good heft to it. Yes, I'm real fond of a good knife."

Dan swallowed, his throat very dry, as he looked at the powerful man.

Chapter 3

"What'd you find?" Cabe called out to Ester from his wagon.

"Bring a light," Ester said.

The oldster opened the bottom part of the Dutch door and stepped outside, moving toward Dan with a lantern.

"Ouch!" Dan bit his lower lip as Ester's hand pressed against his right ankle in an exploratory manner. "Right there's where it hurts, mister."

Ester glanced up at Cabe, saying, "My guess is he has a broken ankle. It's swelled so badly, we'll have to cut off that boot."

The big man looked at Dan. "Any other hurts?"

"Only a headache."

Ester checked Dan's head in the lantern light, nodding. "You've got a lump there on the left-hand side, for a fact. Guess you must've whammed up against something pretty solid. What happened to you? I can

tell by the looks of your ankle that you got
hurt several hours ago."

Dan told them what he remembered about
the gunmen's attack, the details necessarily
sketchy because of his blackout soon after
the wagon had left the road.

"But right now I wish you'd go see about
Uncle Sid," Dan added. "I . . . I don't think
he made it, though maybe he might—"

"Sure, Dan. I'll go right now, uh, just in
case. Cabe, let me have the lantern. While
I'm gone, you might get some water heating
and round up the other stuff we'll need to
take care of this ankle. Dan, you just sit
right here now until we find out a few
things."

Alone a moment later, Dan practically
held his breath at first, then gradually relaxed as he resigned himself to whatever
was inevitable. From where he rested, he
could hear the faint snapping of twigs as
Ester moved about in the ravine, and now
and then he glimpsed a faint glow of lantern
light coming through the brush.

Finally Ester emerged from the ravine,
holding the lantern in front of him. Across
his shoulder a limp form dangled, telling
Dan that his uncle hadn't survived.

Ester and Cabe did what was necessary, carefully wrapping Sid Yeager's body in a tarp and putting it in the lead wagon of Ester's tandem rig.

"We'll take care of the burial in the morning," Ester told Dan. "By the way, one of the mules lived through it somehow or other. She's grazing nearby right now."

"That'll be Judy," Dan said. "I'm obliged to you for going down there to check on things, Ester."

"Had to be done," the big man said simply.

By now Dan had been assisted into Cabe's wagon, where he was sitting in a rawhide-bottomed chair with his right leg propped across an overturned wooden bucket. Looking around, Dan decided he was in a combination cookshack and tack room on wheels. Light was provided by a lamp on a fold-down table. There were a pair of cats on the loose inside, too, at the moment purring against Cabe's pants legs.

"You've been fed twice today," the oldster reminded them. "Go back to your box and let us be here."

Using Dan's own knife, Ester finished cutting off Dan's right boot. Then he examined the ankle.

"It's broken," Ester said. "Cabe, you have everything ready?"

"Whangs are soaking in that hot-water tub on the cookfire," Cabe said. "Those strips of rawhide can mend anything from wagon-wheel spokes to ankles, I reckon. I've also got the corn shucks and strips of bedsheet ready."

"Well, let's have 'em."

Methodically, Ester wrapped a layer of cloth and then a layer of corn shucks around the injured ankle. Then he began completing the makeshift cast with the strips of rawhide Cabe had dipped in the tub on the cookfire.

"This rawhide will dry and do some shrinking, but the corn shucks will keep the cast from getting too tight," Ester said as he continued to work.

He suddenly looked closely at Dan, his intense blue eyes glinting in the lamplight. "You've already told us what happened, Dan. You have any idea why?"

Dan told them about the robbery attempt at the silver shop in San Antonio—how his uncle had shot one of the thieves. "I'm positive those road agents were the same men, Ester. They were getting even with us for that shooting, I suppose."

"Sounds like it. What'd they look like?"

"One of them has an eye that seems to look off to one side, and I heard one of them call him Fluke. But that was the only name I heard. Another fellow was big, with a fringe of reddish whiskers. And the leader wears a hatband buckle shaped like a bear's claw. To me, that one's been the Bear Claw Man since I first saw him in our shop."

"He have a beard?" Ester asked.

"Yes, a thick beard," Dan said.

After exchanging a quick glance with Cabe, Ester said, "You've just described the Jink Barrett outfit, Dan. Reckon they changed their mode of operation when they hit your silversmithy, not that it's out of character. But mainly they've been preying on travelers up an' down this Texas Road for several years now, remaining quite slippery, I might add."

"Rumor has it they buried one of their gang members recently, too," Cabe said, "so that had to be the one your Uncle Sid shot."

"Where were you and your uncle headed?" Ester asked.

"Fort Gibson. Uncle Sid had signed a contract with Jake Lamont, the sulter, for delivery of some merchandise, which I'm sure that Barrett outfit got off with."

"Well, immediately to the south of here there's a lot of open country," Ester mused as he tied the final rawhide strip around the ankle. "So I'd judge that the Barrett gang has headed north up the road. Is Fort Gibson still your destination, Dan?"

"Yes, I want to talk with Jake Lamont, because I've been an apprentice to Uncle Sid for five years, and that merchandise we were delivering was as much my work as it was my uncle's. So, yes, I intend to get to the fort—and I don't intend to arrive there empty-handed if I can do anything at all about it."

Ester grinned widely in the lamplight. "That's the spirit, Dan," he said. "Why, with talk like that, I might even be forced to let you have this Green River knife back."

"I'm not worried," Dan said, having decided that he'd landed among friends by now.

"I've a folding cot I'll fix up for you tonight, Dan," Cabe volunteered, "so you can get your shut-eye right here in the wagon. I've a bed up front where I sleep myself, so you won't be putting me out any."

Cabe rummaged around in the wagon, bringing forth the cot and setting it up, pushing objects back to make room.

As Dan got situated on the cot, resting

the tied-up ankle on a piece of folded-up canvas Ester provided, the latter said, "Don't bang that ankle around any more than you have to during the night, Dan, an' don't forget where you are an' get up during the night an' take a fall outside."

"He'll be just fine, Ester, quit your worrying," Cabe said. "That ankle will hurt like the dickens tomorrow, Dan, but we've done all we can for now. Therefore, I'm calling it quits for the day, since I have to be up early fixin' breakfast. You go on an' do what you want to, Ester."

"I'll hit my bunk as soon as I have a look-see at Jefferson an' the cattle," Ester yawned.

"Jefferson?" Dan asked.

"Allen Jefferson's in charge of my trail crew," Ester said. "The rest of the outfit consists of his helpers, James Spark an' Ike Fort. Then there's my gray dog named Slacker, who also helps with the cattle— my uncle's cattle, actually—a herd of sixty-six this time. And I've got a riding horse called Galahad. He mostly stays with Jefferson's remuda. Anyhow, I'm taking the cattle to the railhead in Falcon City, among other things."

He picked up Dan's knife from the table.

"There's a young stand of bois d'arc near where Jefferson's bedded down the cattle, Cabe. I'll just borrow this knife a little longer, take the lantern, and whomp up Dan some crutches, so he'll have 'em in the morning."

"You never know when to call it a day," Cabe complained good-naturedly. "Where's your own knife?"

"That Arkansas toothpick? I left it on my wagon seat. This Green River knife is much better."

Groggily, Dan squirmed into a more comfortable position on the cot as the talk continued. At the moment he felt tired and whipped. But all the same, as sleep came, his lips pressed together with resolve to have a confrontation with the Jink Barrett outfit as soon as possible. Also, he meant to get back that barrel of silver and deliver it to Jake Lamont at Fort Gibson as his Uncle Sid's contract had stipulated.

Chapter 4

Even though Dan's ankle bothered him off and on during the night, he was able to get some sound sleep, finally awakening at sunup. For a moment he was disoriented, looking around at the wagon's wall shelves, loaded with food and leather-working tools, and at the clusters of onions and garlic hanging about.

Then it all came back to him as he started to get up from the cot, a charge of pain shooting up his right leg when he bumped his new rawhide cast against a chair leg.

Immediately, Cabe was at Dan's side, pressing a hand against his shoulder. "Don't put any weight down on that cast yet, Dan," the old-timer cautioned. "Ester included a little extra buildup on it for a heel, which you can get some use of in a few days. But you'll have to be mighty careful in the meanwhile."

"I wasn't figuring on running a race," Dan joked.

"Yeah—an' you woke up just in time, too, with breakfast waiting for you. Allen Jefferson's two hands have already eaten, and have started hazing the herd on up the road. Well, here's Ester."

The big man appeared at once, framed in the open doorway of the wagon. "Up already, huh, Dan? How's the ankle?"

"Stiff and sore."

"You'll make it just fine. Cabe, hand me those crutches and a chair."

Cabe complied, and Ester helped Dan move outside with the crutches. Then Dan seated himself in the chair Ester had carried out.

Looking at his new cast, Dan said, "You sure those leather strips aren't too tight?"

Ester examined the cast, shaking his head. "That mending bone—the little one at the side of your ankle—will ache and throb for a few days, but gradually you'll be getting back in good shape."

"When can the cast come off?"

"Oh, about the time you start getting used to it." Ester reached inside his boot and returned Dan's knife. "I put an edge on that blade after using it on those crutches."

"Thanks."

A bumping sound came from within Cabe's wagon, and when he started outside with some tin plates and cups, the two cats—one yellow and the other black—leaped across the steps and bounded away, almost causing the oldster to stumble.

"Scat away from here, you two!" he hissed. "Tripping me up like that—I've a good mind to make you both walk today."

"Now you know you wouldn't do that, Cabe," Ester said. "Thorny and Mesquite will be right back there in your wagon when it comes time to go, and you won't try to stop 'em."

"Can't get rid of 'em," Cabe lamented.

"You don't even try."

After Cabe put the utensils on a stump, he plucked a rawhide sack from a hook on his wagon by one side of the Dutch door. He hit the sack on the rim of a wagon wheel, scattering some of its contents, and the cats scampered up and wallowed in the weeds where the wheel rested, playfully fighting with one another and darting here and there beneath the wagon.

"See?" Ester said. "There you go again— an' we have more important things to do than play with cats. Ah—"

The big man faltered, glancing at Dan a little uncomfortably, and the latter sensed what the awkward moment was all about.

"Allen Jefferson an' me an' the other two trail hands took turns with the shovel an' pick, Dan, so we have your Uncle Sid's grave all ready. We'll have the burial right after breakfast, but we better go right ahead with the food now since Cabe has it hot. Speaking of Cabe, we'll be tethering Judy to his wagon in back."

Dan nodded. Under the circumstances, he didn't have any appetite at all, but he realized that other people's lives must go on in spite of what had happened yesterday at the ravine.

Breakfast consisted of sourdough biscuits, gravy mixed with a little hog jowl, and plenty of coffee. During the meal Dan met Allen Jefferson, a dark-complexioned man in his early forties who had unfortunately lost his left hand. There was an iron knob protruding from his shirt sleeve. But the mishap didn't seem to have dulled the man's dexterity in the least as he ate breakfast. He kept a running conversation going during the meal, at one point asking Dan:

"You've been a trail driver, perhaps?"

"No, I've always lived and worked with my uncle. He had a livery stable a long time, but he finally turned to silversmithing."

"Fine, solid trade," Jefferson said. Nodding at Dan's rawhide cast, he added, "I know you'll be glad to get rid of that as soon as possible, Dan. I wasn't so lucky myself, getting shot twice through the arm, having a lot of damage. I felt sorry for myself a while, then got used to it a couple of years back about the time I landed this job with Ester."

A big gray dog trotted up and stopped, watching Dan with his head tilted a little.

"Hello, Slacker," Dan said. "Ester has told me you're good with cattle."

The dog wagged his tail, coming over and sniffing at Dan's footgear, allowing himself to be petted.

"Real steady cow dog," Cabe said, scraping out his Dutch oven into a shallow pan on the ground. "Comes to camp only for something to eat, spending the rest of the day with the cattle."

Slacker made quick work of Cabe's offering, then bounded away without further ado.

While Cabe was engaged with his after-meal chores, Ester handed Dan a rawhide

bag with his Uncle Sid's personal effects.
Dan felt sad as his hand squeezed invol-
untarily at the bag, and he had to fight back
his tears. But he got over the moment, and
shortly thereafter Ester and the other men
lowered the tarp-enclosed body into its
grave. Then, removing his hat, Ester said a
short prayer.

A little later, after an oak sapling cross
had been erected on top of the new grave,
Ester took a final glance toward the ravine
where Sid Yeager's body had been found. He
mentioned that he and Jefferson had pulled
the dead mule to a narrow crevice in the
ravine and covered the animal with rocks.

Then he asked, "Is there anything else
you want from that busted-up wagon down
there, Dan? I already ran across your war
bag with your extra clothes an' things—it's
in my wagon."

Dan shook his head. "No, I'm ready to get
on with what has to be done." The Bear
Claw Man's—Jink Barrett's—image was
becoming more deeply etched in his mind
with each passing minute.

The group started north. Jefferson and his
cowhands stayed ahead with the cattle,
trekking this way and that to accommodate

the traffic up and down the road. Ester trailed along next with his tandem wagons, followed by Cabe's vehicle, the oldster sitting on the right-hand side doing the driving while Dan sat on the left, his broken ankle resting on a gunnysack filled with grass.

Before leaving camp, Dan had a glimpse inside Ester's second wagon, discovering that it was even more of a tack room than Cabe's vehicle. A wide assortment of hides was visible, some on the floor, some hanging up, some of the leather with the hair still on, but most of it with the hair scraped off.

Also, there were a number of newly made harnesses hanging over rawhide lines strung across the interior. The total, Dan knew, represented untold hours of labor.

"What's Ester doing?" Dan asked as Cabe's wagon jostled along behind four high-stepping horses. "Starting a harness shop somewhere up the road?"

"Good guess, Dan," Cabe nodded. "He has a store rented from a Creek family in North Fork Town, about forty miles south of Fort Gibson. That's where one of the branches of the California Road crosses the Texas Road, resulting in a lot of traffic. So where you

have wagons an' such, you have all kinds
of harness repairs and associated needs, an'
Ester means to provide some of it.

"Ester's second wagon has this big thing
with a lot of rawhides sloshing around in
some solution that makes the hair slack off
without too much effort."

"Sounds like an awful lot of work," Dan
said.

"Oh, it is, but Ester thinks he's getting
out of a lot of work by not settling down
someplace. All he knows is goin' up and down
this road, doing all sorts of trading along it
over the years, driving his uncle's cattle to
the railhead. He'll no sooner get his harness
shop set up at North Fork Town than he'll
want to take off on some travel venture
again, just you mark my words."

"You have kinfolk in North Fork Town?"

"No, but we're meeting a close friend of
mine between here an' there. Name's C.L.
High, from over Arkansas way. He's kinda
going in business with us, being a cutler by
trade. He went back home to see about his
stepdaughter, Bete. They should both meet
us about Boggy Depot—or if not, we should
be getting a letter from ol' C.L. when we get
there."

Curious, Dan asked, "How old is this Bete?"

Cabe said, "About your age."

At that instant Dan thought he saw something glint in the distance, but he didn't know what.

Chapter 5

Surprised at seeing Dan Yeager next to the old-timer on the wagon, Fluke-Eye lowered his glinting telescope. Then he quickly fit the telescope into the clamps he'd rigged atop the barrel of his .36 Sharps carbine.

Sprawling in the hot sun atop a huge flat rock among the trees, he judged he was about three hundred and fifty yards from the road where the wagon was slowly moving northward. The Navy Sharps was an old single-shot weapon he had kept because of its uncanny accuracy. If you were careful, one shot was really all it ever took.

Lining up the cross hairs again on his target, Fluke chided himself and the other members of the gang for thinking Dan Yeager was dead.

Obviously, the young silversmith had somehow survived, then been picked up by passing travelers—but the particulars didn't matter.

The important thing was that the young man still lived and was still destined to die because of what had happened back there in that silver shop in San Antonio. Yet just as Fluke was about to pull the trigger, he had second thoughts.

He suddenly grinned and relaxed, knowing he didn't have to rush matters at all. He could pick off his victim any time he chose to.

Well, he would wait, because there was no particular hurry. He would enjoy toying with Dan Yeager, robbing him of sleep and peace.

Jink Barrett would also be pleased to learn that one of their intended victims had survived their initial attack.

This was true because Jink relished stalking a prey as much as he himself did. This would be particularly true under the circumstances because Jink and his cousin, Bert—Fluke's brother—had always been close.

And neither Fluke-Eye nor Jink Barrett would forget how Bert had suffered through those three long days and nights before he died from Sid Yeager's shot.

* * *

Dan was surprised at the great number of horsemen and vehicles they encountered on the road.

It grew hot and still as the day wore on. About one o'clock Allen Jefferson signaled with his hat, and the outfit stopped for lunch and a short rest. Ester and Cabe unharnessed their horses. And while Cabe fixed something to eat, Ester watered the animals at a small stream Jefferson had located, the cattle having plenty of bank space to take on all the water they needed.

There were pinto beans to go with the remainder of the biscuits Cabe had made that morning, in addition to more coffee.

Finishing up a third cup of the strong brew, Cabe said, "Do you think she'll still be there this trip, Ester?"

"I reckon," Ester reflected. "Probably expecting by now, too, unless I miss my guess."

"We'll soon find out."

Dan regarded the pair, neither of whom elaborated. And he found himself with something else to think and puzzle about, not feeling inclined to ask prying questions.

They reached a suitable camping area near the Red River an hour before sundown. Jefferson and his men hazed the cattle over

to a mesquite flat left of the main road, and
Ester and Cabe angled their wagons behind
them. Dan, on the wagon seat with Cabe,
looked ahead and had a good view of the
muddy reddish water.

The sluggish river was wide, more than
two hundred yards, he judged, the water
gurgling along the south bank among the
cattails and scrub willow. Some logs and tree
limbs and leaves were floating out in the
middle.

"Big rains somewhere upstream," Ester
said as he began unhitching his horses. Gazing across the river, he added, "That must
be the ferry over there pulled in at the bank,
an' he's made his last trip for the day. So
tomorrow we'll go ahead an' pay him a dol-
lar apiece to get each of the wagons over,
but Jefferson an' his hands will drive the
herd over for their swimming lesson, because I'm not paying any ten cents each for
those cattle to cross."

"Can't blame you there," Cabe agreed.

Ester stood there with a horse collar in
one hand, now gazing downstream on his
side of the river. Gesturing with his chin,
he said, "But what's that thing I see yonder
through the brush, Cabe? It wasn't there
before."

Cabe and Dan, still seated on the high perch on Cabe's wagon, took a gander in the direction Ester indicated.

"Why, it's got the shape of a riverboat," Cabe observed, "but this is too far upstream for river traffic like that. I bet it was built there to drum up some kind of business— or somebody's gone off his rocker, constructing a house right in the water when there's so much dry land around."

"Could be deserted, too," Ester said, continuing now to unharness his animals.

Knowing he couldn't do much work hobbling around the horses with his crutches, Dan remained on the high seat of the wagon after Cabe scampered down. In the growing dusk a moment later, he happened to be looking in the direction of the "riverboat" when a light was abruptly turned on inside.

"Guess it's not deserted, Ester," Dan said, calling his attention to the light. "Somebody's aboard it, all right."

Cabe glanced up from the cookfire he was starting with some wood he'd taken from a big hide slung like a cradle beneath Ester's second wagon. "Makes a body curious, don't it?" he remarked.

"Soon's we get set up here, I'll have a look-see at it," Ester decided.

"About what I figured," Cabe snorted. "You never have learned to just let well enough alone."

"I reckon not," Ester said.

Chapter 6

As was his wont from time to time, Allen Jefferson sent his two companions into camp for supper while he and the dog watched over the resting cattle. Then he took his turn at eating, bringing Slacker in for something to eat, too.

While Jefferson was partaking of his meal, Ester said, "Allen, you've already made a couple trips up this ol' road with me, helping me get through with a few dozen head of my uncle's cattle each time. But I want you and your men to be extra careful where the cattle are concerned tonight. That old wagon camp a half mile or so from here is probably still as infested with rowdies as ever, and they might be drifting around. You never know."

"Don't worry," Jefferson said. "We'll do you a good job just like you're paying us to do, an' we'll also keep an eye out for the camp here. We'll reach Falcon City with every one of those sixty-six longhorns."

"Fine," Ester said, draining his coffee cup. "I don't have to remind either of us of the lesson I learned with those parasites the last time we came this way. Dropped by their camp I did, like a nitwit, and let myself be talked into a card game with a cheater. Then the whole thing turned into a stupid fight."

"Well, you also have a tendency to lose your patience in card games, Ester," Cabe interjected. "You—"

"Never mind. Just a waste of time, anyway, sitting around on a horse blanket looking at kings an' aces, spades, sixes, an' eights."

"See?" Cabe said with a gleam of triumph in his hazel eyes. "You get your dander up even when you start talkin' about playin' cards."

"Oh, we all have our bad points," Ester said, getting up from his chair.

He glanced toward the riverboat-like structure. "Now, though, I'll go find out what is over yonder an' be right back."

"Don't tarry," Cabe advised. "If I don't see that big ugly face of yours right here in another fifteen minutes, I'll be along to rescue you."

"I admire your confidence in me," Ester

chuckled, patting the revolver at his hip. "No kind of trouble I haven't been able to handle so far, Cabe."

"Just don't go lookin' for trouble too close," the old-timer suggested.

"I know."

As Ester started away, he gave a slight whistle for the dog, and Slacker stopped licking at his food pan and trotted after the big man, the two quickly disappearing into the darkness.

Jefferson returned to the cattle, and Cabe saw to the supper dishes. Ester returned as the old-timer was finishing up, coming through a patch of cattails as the wild cry of a kingfisher pierced the air.

"Aw, dry up," Ester admonished the bird, approaching the campfire with Slacker at his heels. "Nobody's gonna bother your precious nest."

"What'd you find out, Ester?" Cabe asked. "That turn out to be a real boat, after all?"

"No, a kind of loony old former riverboat captain seems to have built the thing there, driving piles down into the riverbed for a foundation, with a long walkway out to it."

"But what's the purpose? Is it a store, or what?"

"No, it's a saloon, mainly," Ester said, grinning at Cabe and then winking at Dan, who was seated on one of Cabe's chairs with his crutches across his knees. "But De Burr—that's the captain's name—does have some foodstuff an' trade goods for sale. Even has a piano there—and, yeah, those smoke stacks were added just for effect, as were a lot of other riverboat features."

"Well, it takes all kinds of different people to keep things humming," Cabe allowed. "So I guess one more party with flightly, crack-brained ideas won't hurt much."

"An' I feel lucky an' in need of a change tonight, Cabe," Ester announced as if on the spur of the moment. "Been a mighty long, dry road up to here, I'm thinking. So dig out a couple of silver pieces from our things, an' I'll buy you a drink."

"Sounds as if you've already had one or two maybe," Cabe said pointedly.

"Just the one, Cabe, and of course it had to be on the cuff, since I don't carry around any cash, which would just wear holes in my pocket anyway, on the road like this. But things did seem to be on the up an' up at De Burr's place, as far as I could tell. I walked up to the bridge leading over to it, talked to a roustabout sort of fellow who suggested that we might as well try to relax a little tonight aboard The Risky Queen since we wouldn't be crossing the river until the morning, anyway. So I thought about it a minute, then said, 'Why not?'"

"Fell for the line just like that, huh?" Cabe accused, snapping a thumb and forefinger. "Let yourself be influenced with the merest hint of suggestion."

Cabe snorted, then began grinning a little, finally shrugging a shoulder. "Well, I don't know," he said. "I suppose we might deserve some relief an' can trust ourselves to go sample the man's brand of poison if we keep on our toes. Jefferson an' the others will be watching over the herd as well as our wagons here, and Slacker will wait under your wagon with a word from you, so let's try it. Wouldn't mind wettin' my whistle myself, now that we've broached the subject."

"Then don't dally. The morning comes mighty early. Let's get going while we're in the mood."

Ester grinned widely. "I knew you'd confirm my sentiments in the matter after a little consideration, Cabe. Be our last night on Texas soil for some time to come. So hurry up an' dig out that silver an' let's board the thing."

Cabe ducked through the Dutch door of his wagon. "Be right with you, Ester. See what Dan wants to do."

The big man turned to Dan, his smile infectious. "Yeah, Dan, how about yourself? That invitation was for you, too, if you feel like making that little jaunt on your crutches with us hide wrestlers. You up to it?"

Dan nodded, thinking that The Risky Queen sounded like a good place to get an updated report on the Jink Barrett gang since the outfit had apparently been heading in this direction.

"I don't intend to just sit here an' rust out while you two have all the fun," Dan said, struggling out of the chair and getting his crutches in place under his arms. "Luckily I had my money on my person when we ran into that trouble, so I'm pulling my own weight in that regard."

"The thought hadn't entered my mind, Dan," Ester said. "You're one of us on this trip, and I'm toying with a proposition I'll discuss with you later. But for right now,

we'll just play things by ear, mix a little fun
with the serious matters, huh?"

"I'm game."

"Don't think I don't know some of the
things that keep spinning through your
mind about what happened, either. I'll back
you one hundred percent when the time
comes to make a move against the Barrett
gang, so don't forget it."

"I've got to clear the Yeager name with
that sutler at Fort Gibson," Dan said. "Uncle Sid had signed a contract to deliver forty-
eight sets of silverware and some other
things."

"I understand, Dan. You'll get your chance
to do what you need to do, and you can count
on me to do what I can."

"I don't expect you to do my fighting for
me, Ester."

"I know you don't. But at the moment
here, this treat's on me, and I want you to
keep your money in your pocket. Besides,
once you take it out, it's gone. You're my
guest tonight—that is, if you can make it."

"I'll make it," Dan said as Cabe stepped
out of his wagon, patting a front pocket to
indicate he had the money.

"Nobody's waiting on me," Cabe said.

"Come on, Dan. Since you're on your feet, I know you're going with us."

Cabe closed both doors on his wagon. Then they started off, Dan learning it was a little difficult negotiating his way in the darkness, hitting ruts from time to time. But each time he faltered, either Ester or Cabe was there at his side with a steadying hand, for which he was grateful.

Presently they neared the walkway that led to the De Burr establishment. Seeing them approach, a man tipped his cap and executed an exaggerated bow, following it up with a wide flourish of his cap to indicate the walkway to their destination.

"Glad to see you back, sir," he greeted Ester amiably. "An' welcome aboard The Risky Queen, each one of you gentlemen." Noting Dan's crutches, he added, "Sorry about whatever accident befell your path, young man, but I trust you're coming along all right."

"It's fine," Dan lied, feeling his ankle throbbing inside its rawhide encasement.

"I'm glad to hear that," the roustabout continued. "So go on along an' pick your poison. Capt'n De Burr is all set up tonight to serve one an' all."

"We intend to try out his fare," Ester said, motioning Dan to the walkway, which seemed to be fashioned over a roped-together string of floating barrels. The saloon was located about twenty-odd yards from the bank.

Dan, moving carefully, started out. Ester and Cabe followed closely, using the handy rope hand-holds on either side of the walk-way.

Once inside The Risky Queen, they found about a dozen patrons ahead of them. Three men stood at a rough pine-board bar. And other customers were scattered about at tables in the huge room, the piano situated at the right-hand side of the bar. A man in a straw hat and fancy purple sleeve garters sat on the piano stool, his nimble fingers trouncing up and down the keyboard quicker than the eye could follow.

But what seized Dan's attention was a set of silverware displayed on a shelf behind the bar. It was from the barrel he and his uncle had been transporting to the sutler at Fort Gibson.

Chapter 7

Dan caught his breath as the contents of the familiar velvet-lined box registered in his brain. And his next reaction was to glance about the place anxiously, searching out any member of the Jink Barrett gang. But among all the strange faces in the room, he didn't see the faces he was looking for.

"You all right, Dan?" Ester asked very softly, sensing something was amiss. "That walk tire you out?"

"No—I'm fine."

"Then let's get on over to the bar and order our drinks. Then I'll pick us out a table."

"Okay."

They moved over to the bar, and Dan assumed that the huge man behind it with hamlike hands had to be the riverboat's captain, De Burr, the man Ester had mentioned. And he was right.

"Ahoy, mates," the man addressed them warmly, giving Ester a lackadaisical salute as he touched his black-visored cap with his hand. "Glad to see you back, sir, not that I doubted for a minute you would return. De Burr's the name, an' riverboating an' trading remains my game. Set your elbows on my bar an' name it, an' I've probably got it: whiskey, brandy, rum, an' beer—room temperature, of course—sarsaparilla, and even sassafras tea if'n you want to wait till I boil up some. Prices right there."

De Burr gestured toward a list on the wall behind him above the liquor shelf. Next to some liquor bottles was the velvet-lined box containing the knife, fork, tablespoon, and teaspoon—carefully made from the best silver—that had been stolen from Uncle Sid's barrel.

But Dan now bided his time, figuring to make his inquiry a little later.

"Or, of course," De Burr added, "I've got coffee in the galley for those who still have the need, though I've noted that most gents are about coffee-logged by the time they get this far from their starting point along the road, be it north or south."

"Well, sounds as if you've got things figured out," Ester said. "Ester's my name an' thirst's my game, so make it a whiskey. You

might as well double it, too, an' save yourself some elbow bending."

"Fair enough," De Burr said, turning to
Cabe. "And you, sir? Your thirst about the
same?"

"Not 'zactly," Cabe said with an air of fake
flamboyance. "I've spent too many years in
Jamaica and points south making horsehair
bridles an' rawhide quirts. So I'll just try
your rum, a double while you're at it."

"A double rum it is, sir." De Burr swung
his glance to Dan. "And you, young man?
What's your pleasure?"

Dan didn't immediately respond because
his gaze was on the silverware set, his mind
going over the possibilities as to how it
wound up aboard The Risky Queen as well
as what had happened to the remainder of
the stolen items.

De Burr addressed Dan a second time,
and if he was following Dan's preoccupied
gaze at the silverware, he didn't let on.

"An' you, young man? Whiskey? Rum?
You made up your mind about your thirst?"

Without reason, Dan felt a premonition
gripping him. There were certain days when
things didn't have the right feel, and this
was turning out to be one of them.

He knew it the instant he heard the scraping noise as somebody moved a chair back at one of the tables in the huge room and said:

"He seems like sassafras tea to me, huh, boys? Not even dry behind the—"

His words were drowned out by the suddenly increased volume of the piano player. But Dan, already on edge, had heard more than enough, and he spun around on his crutches, facing the offending voice, eyeing the big, grinning stranger with his hat pushed back in a cocky manner.

The man felt confident, perhaps, because of the two equally good-sized men at the table with him.

"Only telling it like I see it," the grinning man said innocently enough, as if aching for trouble after spending many days of monotonous travel on the Texas Road. "No sense in stretching the truth."

"You can keep your observations for somebody who might appreciate 'em!" Dan spat back.

"Well, a bristly one we have here," the talker said defiantly. He returned Dan's hard gaze and idly shifted a half-smoked cigar in his mouth. "Let me tell you—"

"Oh, just enjoy your drink, mister," Ester interrupted casually, as if he'd been on this route before. "We've got drinks ordered an' we're still standin' here empty-handed, so you're some ahead of us—but we'll remedy the matter if you let us be."

Turning aside from the intruder, Ester addressed De Burr. "Capt'n, suppose you go right ahead an' fill our order, huh? Dan, what do you want? Name it."

"Double whiskey," Dan blurted without turning his head. "That sounds about right to me." He knew what Ester was doing: trying to avert trouble but not minding risking it, either. But the grinning man's remarks galled Dan, and he himself was not about to back down. Dan had a loose, reckless feeling working inside him and, even though he might be handicapped with the broken ankle, he wasn't above raising a few knots on heads if necessary.

Not that he was looking for a fight here tonight, by any means. He only wanted some answers concerning that set of silverware at the moment.

"Drinks comin' right up," the owner of The Risky Queen said, busying himself with the order.

Dan thought maybe Ester would stand pat and let the troublesome man make the next disparaging remark if he were so minded, but it didn't turn out that way.

Pulling in a deep breath and rocking back on his heels, Ester commented:

"Some people just ain't blessed with any manners at all, are they?"

The utterance was general enough not to bring an immediate response, and Ester motioned to Cabe, who shoved a hand in his pocket after some money as the piano player continued to bear down on his keyboard just in case.

De Burr set the drinks on the bar, took the coin Cabe slapped down, and made change.

"Seventy-five cents for refreshment an' two bits due the customer," De Burr intoned in a businesslike manner, taking the change from a cigar box on a barrel top behind him. "An' there's more firewater where that came from, too. You only have to name it."

Ester nodded, shoving the change in front of Cabe to pocket. "Good," he said, smacking his lips. "But whoa here, I forgot a toast. Red River's gotta be a landmark on our trip, an' we should properly mark the occasion."

"For a fact," Cabe agreed.

Ester raised his glass toward Cabe and Dan, saying, "Here's to a better land awaiting us up the road—an' we'll make it by heck with every bit of our load."

"I'll drink to that," Cabe said.

Ester upped his glass and took a long swig, and Cabe and Dan followed suit, slugging down a mouthful.

Immediately, Dan knew that it had been a mistake, his drink much stronger than the blackberry wine his Uncle Sid used to make from time to time. But he gasped a quick breath and managed to weather the throat-gagging crisis, casually setting his glass back on the bar and getting a better grasp on his crutches.

"Now let's have that table," Ester said, nodding to the only one remaining empty in the place. "No point in your having to stand here all propped up like this, Dan."

"You go ahead, Ester," Dan said. "I'll be right there, but first I want a word with Capt'n De Burr here."

The owner of The Risky Queen snapped his gaze in Dan's direction when Dan said this, his manner at once solicitous. "Yes, lad, what'll it be you wish to speak to me about? The drink all right? If not, I've got—"

"Drink's just what I ordered," Dan said noncommittally. "No complaints."

"I can put a splash of water in it."

Dan shook his head, deciding to approach his subject in an indirect fashion. "I've indicated no problem with the drink, but I'm attracted to that set of silverware there in the box on the shelf behind you. It's mighty fine-looking merchandise—does it happen to be for sale or trade?"

"You have a mighty sharp eye, lad." De Burr smiled, his shaggy mustache inching upward to reveal a gold-capped tooth. "An' of course it's for sale, too. That's honest-to-gosh silver, and it'll last you a lifetime. Twenty dollars will put that set in your back pocket, my friend. You interested?"

"Might be," Dan said without hesitation. "Fact is, I could use a few more sets in addition to that one. Is there more where that came from?"

"Well, I can sympathize with you there, young man, because that's first-quality merchandise," De Burr said genially. "But that's the only set I've got, as a matter of fact."

Dan felt a letdown even though he'd anticipated such a response to his question.

This meant that the Jink Barrett gang was still riding high in the saddle, still in possession of the rest of their stolen merchandise. But Dan had additional questions.

Chapter 8

"Why just the one box?" Dan asked De Burr. "I thought it might be just a sample of what you had stashed away on your riverboat here—perhaps a display set only."

"No, I'm not so lucky," De Burr complained. "I could have had more, but most all my ready cash was tied up in buildin' The Risky Queen, which opened only a couple months back."

"Then someone else has more of the silverware, huh?"

"Oh, yeah, but they're up the road a smart piece by now, I imagine. Fact is, I took that one box there in trade when some gents didn't have the hard cash for drinks. Ah, people must be able to compromise hereabouts, I've learned."

"I suppose."

Sensing that this was about all he would be able to find out from De Burr, Dan came to his decision. Having almost sixty dollars

57

in his possession, he reached for his wallet.

"I have ten dollars here."

"Make it fifteen," De Burr suggested.

"It's a deal."

When Dan completed his purchase, Cabe volunteered, "I'll tote that along for you, Dan, seein's how I can manage a little better."

"Good enough."

After pushing the box of silverware under his waistband, Cabe took his and Dan's drinks over to the table Ester had indicated. He put the drinks on the table, then pulled back a chair for Dan.

"Here, we all need to take a load off—"

Cabe was interrupted as the huge, grinning man who had baited Dan earlier strode up with objections. "Hold it, mister," the man said.

Cabe paused, blinking at the stranger. "What—"

Ester, who had lingered at the bar as Dan made his inquiries about the silverware, left his drink there and moved over to intercede for Cabe. But before he'd taken three steps, the big troublemaker blocked his way.

"Just a minute, fellow," the man said to Ester. "We've some friends comin' this way from the wagon camp, an' we're saving this table for them."

Dan noticed that the whiskey bottle on the man's own table, where his two rough-looking companions were still seated, was almost empty, and he wondered how much that had to do with the big man's behavior. The gent surely did seem determined to start a fracas of some kind, and at the moment Dan wasn't sure how Ester could handle himself.

Ester was big, weighing about two thirty or so, but the grinning stranger was heavier by perhaps twenty-five pounds, and he was also at least half a head taller.

Suddenly on the balls of his feet, Ester wiped the back of his hand across his mouth, glaring at the other man with the faintest hint of a smile. He said, "Now you *really* don't have any manners, do you? This table here's as empty as empty can be, an' if'n you wanted it saved, you should have put up a sign on it or dragged it over someplace for safekeepin', seein's how your friends apparently can't look out for themselves."

"Never you mind my manners," the huge man said. "I'm just tellin' you the facts of the matter. Take it any way you want to."

Idle about his movements, he removed the cigar from his mouth and flipped an ash on the rough floor near Ester's boots.

It was meant as a challenge, but Ester said, "We don't have much time, anyway, mister. Gotta get on back to camp pretty soon an' get some shut-eye for another long haul tomorrow. So, if you don't greatly mind, we'll just have a seat here an' enjoy the rest of our drink. Probably be gone by the time your friends show up."

The huge man grunted knowingly, as though considering that Ester had backed down on the matter. He glanced over to his companions, chuckling deeply in his throat. And when he turned back to face Ester, there was open hostility in his deep-set, round blue eyes.

"Ester, huh?" he sneered, thrusting the cigar stub back into his mouth. "I never did know any man with a woman's name who ever had much grit in his craw. But I reckon Ester is a right pretty name—especially for somebody workin' as a milkmaid or runnin' a nursery back East."

Eyeing the man carefully, Ester said, "There's just one thing you don't know about that you're fixin' to be enlightened on right here an' now, since you refuse to let things stand like they are."

"An' what might that be?" the man asked, planting his cigar at the corner of his mouth and leaving it at a defiant angle. "I'm listening."

"Ester *is* my name, mister, but that's the last part of the handle. Stormy happens to be the front part, which you're going to remember. I was given the latter moniker one time when I was forced to explain the Ester portion to an overly curious gent like yourself more years ago than I care to remember."

The huge man caught his breath, maybe wondering if he'd gone a step too far. But a second later he lunged forward, charging ahead toward Ester, as if to rectify the situation.

Determinedly, he swung a haymaker at Ester, at the same time yelling, "Jobe!"

Jobe, one of the huge man's friends, responded to the summons and got up from the table, withdrawing a revolver from his holster. Ester, who'd evaded the first blow, ducked under another haymaker and slammed a fist up hard against his opponent's chin.

From the edge of his vision, Dan saw old Cabe unleash a rawhide quirt dangling from his belt and pop the leather snapper down hard against Jobe's hand, causing the latter to yowl out in pain as his more deadly weapon dropped on the table, where it spun around and knocked a drink in the lap of the third would-be troublemaker, who tripped over backward in his chair.

Moving quickly, Cabe retrieved the revolver on the table.

"Dangerous weapons, these things," the old-timer said, putting away his quirt and cocking the revolver, covering the pair of troublesome accomplices. "So now that it's mine, you two just hold everything right where you have it. For all I know, this hogleg's liable to have a hair trigger. What do you think?"

Cabe started to bear down on the trigger, and the pair froze in their positions, respecting Cabe's warning, not choosing to chance further action.

"That's better," Cabe said, continuing to brandish the revolver.

Ester's opponent spat out his now-broken cigar, his eyes glazing with resoluteness as he gathered his strength to take another swing at Ester's head.

"Gentlemen, take your troubles ashore!" Captain De Burr admonished. "I'm still paying for settin' up here for you travelers, and I don't want things busted up, if you don't mind."

The piano player stopped playing, shutting the keyboard lid, turning his attention to the fight as Ester elbowed away his opponent's punch and grappled with the man, moving the larger fellow toward the saloon entrance.

"The Capt'n says to take the fight out of here, mister," Ester grunted as he forced the huge man out to the walkway. "I suppose we might as well oblige him—don't you think?"

The other man had but one recommendation: "Don't!"

But Ester paid him no mind at all, dragging him across the walkway.

Like several of the bystanders, Dan moved toward the entrance to see how the fight would end. But as he started outside, a slump-shouldered man from one of the other tables grasped his elbow, and Dan looked around.

"I've a comment for you, mate," the man said confidentially.

"What is it?" Dan wondered as others pushed by.

"We don't know one another, an' maybe you already know what I'm about to say," the slump-shouldered man continued. "But I like the way you handle yourself, and I could tell you've got more than a casual interest in the silverware because I was here earlier when De Burr took it in trade. I was sitting at a nearby table when a certain crazy-eyed gent I've known of for years dropped a hint on how he and his friends had come upon certain goods.

"A lot of stealing goes on up an' down the road, so I put two and two together when you started asking De Burr those questions. Well, I hate to bear ill tidings, but you might as well kiss the rest of that load good-bye— because *nobody* has ever wrested anything back from that riffraff bunch who stole your goods."

Chapter 9

As soon as the slump-shouldered man finished talking to Dan, he whirled and disappeared ınto the darkness outside The Risky Queen, giving the impression he didn't want to become any more involved in someone else's problems. A little taken aback but not completely overwhelmed at the man's pronouncement about the Jink Barrett gang's invincibility, Dan followed the fellow outside, wanting some more words with him.

But by the time Dan hobbled through the entryway, the man was already half across the walkway. Meanwhile, Ester was still wrestling with the huge stranger, getting ready to push him into the river.

"In you go—"

"I can't swim!" the stranger said.

It was too late for Ester to respond to the announcement even if he'd wanted to. The other man was already flailing the air with his arms before hitting the water with a tremendous splash.

"Now look at what you've done," Ester grumbled good-naturedly. "Got me good an' wet!"

"But not half as wet as *he* is, sounds like," Cabe guffawed, still inside but craning his neck to look out the doorway. Then Cabe said:

"Can't swim?"

He glanced at the table where he was covering the pair with his borrowed revolver, addressing the one who'd a moment ago toppled backward with the drink in his lap. "If you put your hardware down on the table top real easylike, you and your friend here might go outside to see about your drinking partner. Think you can manage that?"

The man nodded eagerly. "We better because Lakin can't swim a lick, for a fact."

He put his six-gun on the table as Cabe had instructed, and the two of them hurried outside to the rail of the walkway.

In the dim light thrown out by a lantern, Dan saw the erstwhile troublemaker struggling and fighting in the water, churning and heaving this way and that. Then, discovering that the water was no more than waist deep, the huge man regained enough of his composure to stop sputtering and splashing. Instead he grabbed his hat, which had started to float downstream.

"You're lucky that I didn't land that first punch a while ago," he snarled at Ester as he emptied the water from his hat and slammed it down on his head. "You'd still be countin' stars."

"You want to try again?" Ester said.

"Well, I—"

Ester hooted with raucous laughter. "You didn't even come close, mister," he said. "I've ducked better ones than that in my sleep. An' on your next go-around, if you're so foolish, you might be more careful an' don't let a person's name trick you like that."

The man rubbed his jaw thoughtfully, returning Ester's easy stare. "All right, let's leave it be. I know when not to press my luck—which I was mighty short of just now. You pack a right mean wallop when you want to."

"So let's just forget it," Ester said as the dripping man climbed onto the walkway with the help of his companions.

"I'll be glad to."

Ester didn't push his advantage, nor was he a man to hold a grudge. "An' now that we're still here this close, we might as well go back inside for another drink," he decreed. "That's what we came here for, right?"

"You've hit it solid center," the bigger man said, still spitting water.

The piano player picked up where he'd left off on his keyboard as one and all reassembled inside De Burr's riverboat saloon to finish their drinking.

Dan and his new friends returned to their camp within the hour, Ester leading the way. Dan had been doing some heavy thinking about the appearance of the all-too-familiar silverware, and right after they reached their campsite, Ester spoke up, echoing the slump-shouldered man's comments in The Risky Queen.

"That set of silverware you bought back there from De Burr—you'd seen its likes before, huh?"

Dan sat down in the chair Cabe made ready for him. "Guess that proves my questions weren't the least bit discreet, Ester."

"How's that?"

Dan relayed the remarks of the slump-shouldered man, then added, "Of course I'd seen that silverware before. Uncle Sid and I made up forty-eight identical velvet-lined boxes of sets like this one we brought back with us tonight. The silverware was the main part of the load we were hauling in our wagon to the sutler at Fort Gibson. The rest of the stuff was just some wind chimes, earrings, candlesticks, an' things like that."

"I'd figured as much," Ester said. "So we all know now that the Jink Barrett outfit is up the Texas Road ahead of us. Already crossed over the river on the ferry, in all likelihood, and on the watch to dispose of your silverware as well as any other merchandise they might have picked up from others along the way."

"I realize it," Dan said, gratefully resting his aching ankle across an ancient, beat-up ottoman Cabe brought out of his wagon. "I just wish—"

"I know," Ester cut in, as if delving into Dan's thoughts. "You'd like to take one of our horses and rush up the road so you can tangle with the Jink Barrett outfit an' settle matters once an' for all. But if you did that, I'd just have to follow you, so who'd drive my wagon? Jefferson needs two flankers an' himself to handle those longhorns, an' Cabe has his own rig to see to. What I'm gettin' at, Dan, is that I don't want you doing something foolish. Promise?"

What Ester had said about borrowing a
horse and riding off had been at the edge of
Dan's thinking, but he knew how unfair it
would be for him to do that.

He nodded. "You've got my word, Ester.
But—"

"Just hold it right there, Dan," Ester cautioned. "I know how you feel about this matter, and I predict we'll get our whack at the
Jink Barrett outfit before our trip's over.
They'll pull some boner or other, an' when
they do, we'll be all over 'em. But for a while
let's just bide our time, give yourself enough
rest to get that ankle on the mend."

What Ester had said made sense, but it
didn't help Dan get to sleep on the pallet
beneath Cabe's wagon. The pallet idea was
his own, since he'd found sleeping inside the
wagon the night before rather warm.
Though the outdoor pallet was more comfortable, he lay there for a long while, al-
ternately closing and opening his eyes as
sleep evaded him and Cabe's two cats stalked
shadows in the moonlight. However, sleep
finally came.

The group was up early the next morning,
utilizing the ferry to get the wagons over
the river. Jefferson and his hands swam the

herd across the muddy red water without incident.

That evening they pitched camp near a small stream. Trouble came roughly an hour after supper, while Cabe was busy inside his wagon on a harness-stitching rig and Ester was lingering near the cookfire sipping coffee.

A spurting thump of noise hissed in the cookfire, and almost simultaneously from some undetermined distance away in the darkness came the blast of a rifle. Ashes scattered, and red-hot coals hopped and rolled on the ground, setting tiny twigs and dry grass afire right beside Ester's left boot.

Dan snapped fully awake on his pallet beside a wheel of Cabe's wagon. He knew immediately what was going on. The Fire-Shooter was on his tail again.

Chapter 10

Spattered with ashes, Ester dropped his tin cup and knocked over the coffeepot in his haste to get away from the cookfire.

"Douse your light, Cabe!" Dan instructed as he scampered beneath the old-timer's wagon, careful with his broken ankle. "An' stay back from the fire, Ester!"

The big man rolled underneath the wagon beside Dan, exhaling a gust of air. "Sounds as if you've been through this exercise before, Dan."

"I have."

Ester peered into the darkness. "Need I ask what it's all about?"

"The shots usually come in threes," Dan explained, "though the Fire-Shooter did break his pattern a time or two."

"Fire-Shooter?"

"Yeah, that's what Uncle Sid and I nicknamed whoever it was that started shooting up our camp soon after we left San Antonio.

We finally decided it might be connected with a vengeance plan by the gang who tried to rob our silver shop earlier, but we never knew for sure."

"You could've been right, Dan," Ester said, looking through the wheel spokes. "Cabe, you got your light out in there?"

"Yeah, I do."

The second slug tore through the ashes, clanging against Cabe's Dutch oven and ricocheting off a wagon-wheel rim, and whining into the distance. Then quickly came the loud, hollow-like blam of the firearm responsible.

"What's it all about?" Cabe yelped from above.

"We'll explain later," Ester said. "For now, though, just try to get behind something solid."

A moment of silence followed, interrupted finally by a third shot, which thumped harmlessly into the dying fire, showering a handful of sparks and ashes on the dry grass. Using one of Dan's crutches, Ester raked dirt over the small candle-like blazes.

Presently he said, "Well, that was number three, so maybe we're off the hook for the rest of the night."

"One sequence of shots was all we ever went through at a single time," Dan said.

"So we'll hope that's it for this time," Ester said. "At least the cattle didn't get spooked. And since nobody was hit, I suppose we got off lucky."

"It makes me wonder if the Jink Barrett outfit learned I'm still alive and got taken by you and Cabe," Dan said. "Surely they wouldn't have shot at your camp at random, would they?"

"Well, I just don't know, Dan," Ester said thoughtfully. "Maybe whoever it is just wants to keep in practice."

"I'm bringing you trouble, Ester," Dan said. "You didn't know what you were taking on when you helped me—and I didn't know, really, that I'd still be plagued like this. Maybe I better—"

"Maybe you better let me worry some about it," Ester said. "Cabe claims I'm good about worrying—but sooner or later I'm also good about doing something about it. So let me take the burden of this now, since it's my camp an' you're my guest."

Suddenly silence once more engulfed the night and the land around them. Dan, thinking back on that fateful day in the silver shop and the glimpse he'd had of the gunmen before his uncle's wagon sailed down the ravine, wondered which one was continuing the target practice. The man with the reddish whiskers didn't strike him as a likely suspect, and neither did the leader, Jink Barrett.

So that left Fluke-Eye. Dan tried to remember whether he'd glimpsed a long-barreled weapon in Fluke's hand after his Uncle Sid had been shot. But for the life of him, he wasn't sure.

One of the longhorns bawled out, and Cabe came out of his wagon.

"I trust everybody is all right, aren't you?" the old-timer asked.

"Oh, we're doing just fine," Ester answered, rolling out from under the wagon. "Just another demonstration, from what Dan has been telling me."

"Well, we can do without that," Cabe said.

Ester mentioned what Dan had said, adding, "Since it's liable to happen again, too, we better start building our cookfire a little farther away from your wagon, Cabe, just to be on the safe side—not that it would help a lot if the gent insisted on getting serious. But I think right now it's only a nuisance thing, just to keep us on edge."

"That sort of thing would certainly do the trick," Cabe said, carefully easing over to the ashed-over cookfire. "I only hope my Dutch oven weathered the storm—"

The old-timer found his pot intact and left it where it was, in position for use the next morning. Dan took his pallet beneath Cabe's wagon for the remainder of the night. Ester brought over a rawhide ground cover and slept nearby.

Surprisingly, Dan fell promptly asleep. His dreams were peaceful until images of the Jink Barrett gang began to trouble him.

When Dan opened his eyes, Cabe had breakfast on the cookfire. Jefferson and his two trail hands had already eaten. Less than forty minutes later, they were on the road again, heading north.

For the next few nights no one shot at Dan and his friends. He was heartened by that and the fact that his ankle was feeling better.

But the peace was not to last. The night they camped along a shallow creek at the edge of the Choctaw Nation, Dan was awakened by a bullet's splat. It came from the cookfire.

He banged his head against the running gear of Cabe's wagon as he automatically started to sit up on his pallet.

Chapter 11

Dan rubbed his head, feeling the start of a lump where he'd clunked it on Cabe's running gear.

"You okay, Dan?" Ester called from his own wagon.

"Just fine."

"Cabe?" Ester said.

"I'm all right and my lamp's out," the old-timer said, "but he caught me right in the middle of a good tale in one of my old magazines."

"It'll keep."

The second bullet struck the cookfire—which Cabe had built about thirty feet away from his wagon—plopping a small spew of fiery matter in the grass and clanking into a tin can, which Cabe had left in the dying coals. The remote blam of the firearm sounded a fraction of a second later and, strangely, Dan heard Cabe chuckle.

"You gone plumb loco in your old age?"

Ester demanded as a blob of moon overhead blinked through a layer of clouds. "What in the dickens can be funny, Cabe? What're you seein' fit to cackle about when it comes to gettin' shot at?"

"Oh, I just tried to give that ninny with the rifle a little false satisfaction, and I think I might have succeeded, that's all."

"Meaning what?" Ester asked in an impatient, hushed voice.

"That so-called Fire-Shooter must have heard the clink of his bullet hitting that tin can I planted in the cookfire," Cabe pointed out, "so I bet he thinks he's ruined my coffeepot or some other necessary utensil."

"I see what you mean," Ester intoned with grudging tolerance. "Maybe it worked."

The expected third shot zanged out, thumping in the cookfire coals stirred up by the first two shots.

"That fellow must have real sharp eyes," Cabe murmured. "Got a real accurate firearm in his hands, too."

Cabe's words were interrupted by the sound of spooked cattle pounding their collective hoofs across the rough terrain.

"Let 'em go an' just hold your positions a while," Ester advised. "Jefferson an' his men will see to the longhorns, an' I don't want either of you unnecessarily tempting that fellow out there with the ready trigger finger. I wouldn't even relight that lamp of yours tonight, Cabe."

"At this rate I'm liable to never get that story finished," Cabe grumbled.

"It's just too bad," Ester said. "But at least this way you'll live to tell about what you did read."

"Still, I'd like to—"

Cabe's comment was cut short by an additional shot from the stalking Fire-Shooter, and this time the bullet struck the canvas covering Cabe's wagon.

"Now that one's gettin' a little too close to home," Cabe readily admitted. "Ah, you don't have to convince me now about not lighting up my lamp, Ester."

Crouching low, as heavier clouds obscured the area, Ester raced from his own wagon and joined Dan beneath Cabe's, flopping flat on the ground.

"I knew sooner or later the Fire-Shooter would break that three-shot pattern you mentioned, Dan."

"Yeah, an' he's not restricting himself to our cookfire, either," Dan said. "But do you think Cabe might be safer down here with us?"

"Oh, chances are about the same, I guess," Ester said. "He has a lot of bins and drawers containing cans with corn an' tomatoes, an' other stuff, so that, plus the wooden bed of the wagon, should make it safe enough in there, if he keeps hunkered down, that is." He turned his head to the wagon. "You are keeping down, huh, Cabe?"

"Wouldn't be caught no other way in such circumstances," Cabe replied. "But I'll have some holes to patch in that canvas over-head, an' that bullet clipped some twine I had a bunch of dried onions hanging from."

"We can weather that kind of damage," Ester said.

Still another bullet whanged against a wheel of Ester's rig and spun off into the night.

"Another nuisance attack," Ester said with disgust. "Trying to keep us stirred up an' on edge, making up for some of the nights he's missed."

The rumbling sound of the stampeding cattle sounded a little different, and Dan had the feeling that the herd was beginning to circle, maybe due to the hazing tactics of

Jefferson and the others. Then, a moment later, another bullet found their cookfire.

"I bet that fellow knows this road like the back of his hand," Cabe said from above, "every depression, ravine, an' hole in the ground between here an' the Rio Bravo. He's got our address, an' he's not goin' to let us forget it."

"I know," Ester said, patting at his right hip, as if to insure that his Colt was still there. "An' I don't intend to sit still for it. You two keep down, you hear?"

With that admonition, Ester scrambled to his feet, loping, in what seemed to be a roundabout way, toward the source of their trouble.

"He's bound to get himself killed one way or another," Cabe predicted from the rear part of his vehicle. "Never can just let well enough alone, wantin' to tangle with the very devil." He looked out toward the darkness. "Ester, you be careful out there."

Cabe's words of caution were spoken in a hushed tone, as if he were afraid to tempt fate by speaking too foolishly loud.

Then, as if in afterthought, Cabe added, "Now, Dan, don't *you* try anything nonsensical. Just stay put, as Ester suggested.

I know how you young bucks can be."

"I couldn't overtake a turtle with these crutches, Cabe, so don't worry."

"Just because the notion hasn't yet struck you," Cabe said thoughtfully.

Dan propped his head against a rear wagon wheel, the contact bringing ground reverberations of the spooked longhorns. For a few heartbeats, Dan didn't move, just remained listening and waiting.

But there were no more shots, and presently some nearby whippoorwills started calling to one another again, and the cookfire was completely fuzzed over with dead ash. Yes, the rumble of the longhorns was getting closer, apparently drifting back toward the original bed-ground.

"Too bad that distance those cattle put behind them just now couldn't have been straight up on the road to North Fork Town," Cabe said, stepping from the Dutch door of his wagon. "But nobody's hurt, so I guess we might as well count our blessings, right?"

"I suppose," Dan agreed.

One of the cats pounced from the shadows and wrapped its tail about Cabe's ankle.

"By yourself, Mesquite? Where's Thorny?"

"I sure hope Ester's all right," Dan said a moment later.

"Me, too," Cabe said.

Chapter 12

A moment later the second cat bounded up and rubbed its head against Cabe's pants leg.

"Well, Thorny, I see you made it through the firing exercise," the old-timer said. "Now we'll all see if we can't get through the rest of the night. Sure puts the hamper on me, though, not being able to use my lamp— can't do any more nighttime reading, nor can I finish that rawhide quirt I started the other day."

"The days just aren't long enough for you and Ester, are they?" Dan asked as he tried to get comfortable on his pallet once more. "Always have another chore to do."

"Oh, I guess it's all we know," Cabe mused. "This old road's become our home, I guess you'd say. We just don't know any different."

Preoccupied with the possible danger that Ester might be in, Dan had a difficult time getting back to sleep. But he finally managed it.

Stretching and yawning the next morning, Dan kept his head low so he wouldn't bump it against Cabe's running gear again. Between the wheel spokes, he saw Cabe by himself at the cookfire, stirring something in the Dutch oven.

"You up all night?" Dan asked.

"Most of it," Cabe said. He nodded to the edge of the clearing where Ester was emerging on his mount, Galahad. "But I surely didn't know when Ester came back here to saddle up an' then take off again. I reckon maybe he's been helping Jefferson an' the others with those longhorns. About the time you think you've got 'em settled down, they get skittish all over on account of nothing, it seems."

Ester rode up, sniffing at the air. "I'll have to say that breakfast smells extra good this morning, Cabe. Last night just about wore me out."

"Well, it's about time for a report from you," Cabe said, a mixture of relief and curiosity in his voice. "Where've you been, an' what's gone on? We were expecting you back hours ago. Did you track down that Fire-Shooter?"

Dismounting and leaving Galahad ground hitched, Ester got a cup and helped himself to some coffee. "I'll just have to sort those questions out," he said, nodding at Dan as the latter rolled out from beneath Cabe's wagon and pulled his pallet after him.

"Yeah, what about the Fire-Shooter?" Dan echoed. "You learn anything about him?"

Ester squatted on his heels, sipping at his steaming coffee. "No, he'd already slunk off by the time I got out to where he'd been laying for us. But in the meantime, I've helped Jefferson an' his hands with those longhorns.

"Now I didn't find out anything helpful there where the Fire-Shooter has been. Just some boot tracks, which didn't mean anything because I'd never seen them before—though I would recognize 'em again, mind you. But that was all the evidence he left this time—he must have even pocketed his empty cartridges."

"Being the extra neat sort," Cabe scoffed.

"Yeah, an' he stood at a sapling with his rifle barrel resting in a fork, which didn't hurt his accuracy, I suppose. But maybe next time I can get out there to him before he ups an' takes off."

"We don't need any blamed next time," Cabe snorted. "But what we want an' what we get will probably be two different things."

"You're right there," Ester agreed.

Dan put his crutches beneath his armpits and got to his feet, a little disappointed that Ester had learned so little. But at the same time he was glad that the big man hadn't run into something he couldn't handle. Dan thought the excitement of the previous night would have taken his appetite, but he was mistaken, the aroma of Cabe's early-morning efforts tantalizing him as he worked the stiffness from his limbs by taking several steps back and forth beside the wagon.

"How's the ankle?" Ester asked, eyeing his handiwork with a critical glance. "Feel better?"

"Not bad at all this morning," Dan said, continuing his practice steps.

"Well, you can begin putting a little weight on that heel pretty soon," Ester said. "Still, don't try to rush things too much."

"I won't."

Ester sipped at his coffee, nodding toward a faint nearby rise. "Jefferson and his men have the cattle fairly settled an' grazing just over that ridge there, Cabe. I think I'll just let 'em feed there on the grass this morning without being in a big hurry to strike out. Soon's I grab a bite to eat, I'll go have a look at 'em again, make sure everything's all right.

"But I notice that rawhide pouch beneath my second wagon's getting close to being empty of firewood, so we better see to a little more this morning while we have a chance."

"Yeah, we'll be needing a little more firewood real soon now," Cabe agreed. "But I'll take care of that while you an' the others keep an eye on those frisky animals."

At that moment Dan remembered a likely deadfall he'd seen nearby in a gully off to one side.

"But you will have to be extra careful with the cattle, Ester," Cabe went on. "Once they get used to stampeding like that, sometimes the least little noise will start 'em off once again. An' that gets to be no fun on a long trip like this."

Dan sat down in the chair at the rear of

Cabe's wagon and put his crutches aside as
the old-timer handed him a tin plate with
gravy and biscuits.

"That should hold you for a while," Cabe
said.

"Looks good," Dan said, digging into the
food.

"Which reminds me," Ester said, loading
his own tin plate, "I'll pick us up a real fine
smoked ham when we get to Boggy Depot
like I usually do, Cabe. That'll supplement
that slab of hog jowl hanging in your wagon."

"It'll be about time, too, because I'm having to do some fancy thin slicing on that
jowl to make it stretch," Cabe said.

"So I've noticed."

"Now don't start criticizin' the cook, Ester!"

The big man grinned, recognizing a touchy
subject with the old-timer. "Wouldn't dream
of doing that, Mr. Cabe Vesta."

Dan realized it was the first time he'd
heard mention of Cabe's last name. Which
reminded him that he'd not known of the
"Stormy" portion of Ester's name until a moment before that fight aboard The Risky
Queen. And it occurred to Dan that the two
men did an awful lot of talking while ac-

tually remaining mighty closemouthed about themselves.

Jefferson and the trail hands came up one at a time to have breakfast. Then the gray cow dog, Slacker, trotted in for something to eat.

"So we'll just noon it right here?" Cabe asked Ester at one point.

"Yeah, it'll give those trail horses a much-needed rest after that racing around last night," Ester said.

"Don't be surprised if'n you have a skimpy second breakfast today then," Cabe decided. "Be a little short of flour by the time we get to Boggy Depot, too."

"Oh, we always make out somehow," Ester said.

A moment later he was back astride Galahad, clucking for Slacker to follow as they started off to check on the grazing cattle.

Getting hold of his crutches, Dan hoisted himself up from the chair, saying, "Are you predicting your friend, C. L. High, will be alone when he joins us at Boggy Depot or up the road?"

The old man smiled. "You're dwelling on it, aren't you?"

"On what?" Dan asked.

"On C. L.'s adopted daughter, Bete, that I mentioned, that's what. Well, I just don't know, Dan. She's about as strongheaded as they come, got the blackest eyes you ever saw on anybody, along with a dusty sprinkle of freckles across her nose, an' she's growing up in a big hurry. But for all I know, she might even be married by now, and C. L. could be by himself. We'll have to bide our time and see. Oh, I share your anticipation—but maybe for different reasons."

"Well, I'll go get some firewood," Dan said, getting a better grip on his crutches. "I saw some not far from here."

"You sure you're up to it?"

"I know I am."

"That's what you think," Cabe said. "You can't carry much of anything while you're on crutches, Dan, unless it's in a sack. And firewood is big and heavy."

"I'll make out somehow," Dan said. "At least I can get some located, bring a little back, and make several trips—"

"Okay, you go ahead, if it's your pleasure to try it. I can lend you a hand later, but first I've a chore or two to attend to."

"I'll be back shortly, Cabe," Dan said, angling into a clump of mesquite on one side of the road.

Moving along carefully, Dan had to watch where he was placing his crutches, not wanting to stick them into any hidden roots or the like.

Chapter 13

Dan was about to pick up a stick of wood, then paused, realizing he couldn't carry much of anything, just as Cabe had said. But he got an idea. He decided to hunker down and free one piece of wood at a time from the deadfall, then toss the pieces over the ridge separating him from camp. Steadying himself on his knees and one of the crutches, he worked loose several pieces of firewood with his left hand.

Presently, as he started to whirl around and toss the first piece of wood over the ridge, a sort of premonition made him hesitate, telling him to be careful.

Straining his ears, he heard a faint mumble of voices back where Cabe was supposed to be by himself. There seemed to be three people at the camp now, including Cabe. Dan couldn't distinguish any of the words, though. Guardedly, he put the piece of fire-

wood back on the ground, then turned toward the ridge, careful not to make any
noise.

There was something about Cabe's clear-
pitched voice that sounded like a warning
to Dan—a signal for him maybe to conceal
his presence from the men the old-timer was
talking to.

Gingerly, Dan put down his crutches and
wiggled up the ridge, keeping behind brush
and clumps of grass so he couldn't be spotted
by anyone around the wagons. Squinting
through the greenery, he saw two mounted
men with Cabe and, luckily, the pair had
their backs to the ridge where Dan was po-
sitioned.

Now the voices became plain enough to
understand.

"Looks like we might be just in time for
dinner," one of the mounted men observed.

"It's a late breakfast I'm fixing," Cabe answered, his voice still clearer than usual, a
skillet in one hand.

Dan, knowing he couldn't be seen at the
moment by the pair of uninvited visitors,
hazarded a slight wave with his right hand
to let Cabe know he didn't have to put on
any more acting for his benefit. He, Dan,

wasn't about to show himself to the new-comers.

"Breakfast *this* time of day?" the second man scoffed. "You right sure this ain't dinner?"

"Decidedly sure," Cabe said. He returned to his natural tone of voice, and Dan knew the old-timer had gotten his message. "Breakfast comes any time during the day I decide on it, since I'm the cook."

"Comin' up from down the trail?" the second man asked while craning his neck and trying to see what might be in the wagons. "Ah, we thought we heard some cattle running, too. Figured to drop by to ask if you needed any help."

"We've got everything under control now," Cabe said.

"Cattle all settled down, huh?" The man rose in his stirrups a little as if to get a better look into Cabe's Dutch door, which happened to be closed at the bottom.

"Far as I know." Cabe nodded. "But it's the others' job to take care of them—over that rise there, if you want to take a look-see."

"Oh, I don't think I care to do that," the man said with what seemed a deceptively lazy tone. "It may be that I can see all I'm interested in right here in your camp."

The man turned his head—and Dan caught his breath as he recognized him. The thick beard was missing, but the giveaway bear's claw on the hatband was still in evidence. This was none other than Jink Barrett himself, the leader of the gang that was so determined to see him dead.

Barrett pulled his gaze around then, gesturing with his chin toward Ester's tandem rig. "I see plenty of wagons around here, but nobody except yourself watchin' over things. Where've you run everyone off to?"

The other rider chuckled, holding a carbine at the ready. "Yeah, this might very well prove interesting," he speculated, "especially to you, old man."

His last two words were laced with contempt, as if he was just about ready to harm Cabe.

But Cabe Vesta didn't budge; he just stood there with the skillet in hand, glaring up at the two men as if daring them to make an unwise move. Finally clearing his throat, he said:

"Gentlemen, you don't know what or who might be there inside my wagon, or in the tandem setup over there. An' I must say, that fellow we picked up down the road is sure handy with a rifle. You may not, of course, even have a notion of what I'm talking about, or have the least reason to be concerned..."

Cabe's bluff was something for them to think about, all right. There surely wasn't any way for the pair to determine whether he was telling the truth. There could very well be a person in one of the wagons drawing a bead on them.

"Where you gents heading?" Cabe asked, pressing his initiative. "Fine day for traveling."

"Maybe yes, maybe not," Jink Barrett said. "One never knows what he might meet up with on this stretch of road, trouble lurking here an' there like it seems to do most every day."

"I know what you mean," Cabe said.

Dan made sure he was well concealed by brush as Barrett's companion with the strange left eye turned his head.

"Hey, what's that over yonder?" Fluke-Eye said, peering in Dan's direction. "Something over there moved. I'm almost certain."

"Nothing," Jink Barrett said with a trace

of annoyance. "My bet says that the old man here's alone."

"I'm not too sure about that," his companion said. "I've just got the feelin' we're being watched."

"Forget it. We've got more important things to do—maybe right here."

"But I did see something move," Fluke insisted.

"Oh, you're always seein' things, conjuring up more trouble than a cavalry troop could handle."

Fluke slapped his carbine with disgust. "Of course, you didn't see anything, Cousin. But you weren't lookin' where I was, either."

"Could be reinforcements on the horizon," Cabe suggested mildly.

Jink Barrett snorted, shaking his head as his right hand went to the revolver at his hip. "I think not."

"Sorry you gents have to move along," Cabe said, edging his free hand toward the quirt fastened to his belt.

Fluke-Eye reined his dun toward the old-timer. "Don't try anything fancy there, mister."

"Only want to keep the fire tended to," Cabe said. "Being the cook, I've got work to do." He went ahead and saw to his cookfire.

Fluke-Eye didn't say anything for a moment, and neither did Jink Barrett. For Dan, the world seemed to grind to a halt as he remained flat against the ground.

Turning his glance in Dan's direction again, Fluke-Eye said, "It just moved out there, Cousin."

As Dan tried to flatten himself even more, something to his left made a slight noise. Then a young cottontail rabbit jumped up and sprang away, apparently frightened.

Fluke-Eye grunted. "A blasted rabbit, Cousin. Well, I knew I'd seen something out there."

"I'm impressed," Jink Barrett said, turning back to Cabe. "So much for reinforcements, old man. You've been running a bluff on us, but now it's time to get down to the purpose of our visit."

Chapter 14

With utmost caution, Dan raised his head a little. Jink Barrett, his hand on his revolver, studied the old-timer before him.

But, regardless of the menacing attention Cabe was getting, he refused to be intimidated, saying, "If you want trouble, just keep pushing at me like this an' you'll have it."

"You're the one to be worrying," Barrett advised.

Abruptly the sound of an approaching horse came from the north. "What's that?" Fluke-Eye blurted, glancing around.

All three of them peered in the direction of the noise.

"Just what I was afraid of," Jink Barrett said. "It'll be getting a little too crowded here right pronto. That looks like the head of this outfit."

As Dan took a peek through the brush, he could tell that the rider heading for their campsite was Ester.

"We might drop in on you later, mister," Jink Barrett told Cabe.

"All set to take care of an old man, huh?" Cabe snapped at him. "But now somebody's coming to spoil your fun. Well, don't go runnin' off before the meal's ready."

"Oh, come on, Fluke," Jink Barrett said irritably. "Let's move outta here." He wheeled his horse, heading for protective brush along the east side of the road. "We've got our own place to take our vittles, an' other fish to fry. Besides, the smell of this cookin' here makes me want to throw up."

Cabe came alive at the insult, freeing his quirt and snapping it against his pants leg. "Hurry back any time you want your ears set back a notch or so," he challenged. "I'll be more than willing to oblige."

Fluke-Eye's dun was a little slow starting, and Cabe lashed its rump, making the animal jump before it came under control.

"Now git!" Cabe snarled. "Both of you! An' I'll be ready the next time you think you can bully an old man!"

"I'll show you right now," Fluke-Eye retorted. But as he started to level his carbine, Jink Barrett stopped him.

"Not here right now, Fluke. We'll bide our

time a little." Glancing at Cabe, the gang leader added, "You ain't seen the last of us— I'll guarantee it."

Then he and his companion cleared out in a rush, both their mounts kicking up dirt.

With the pair gone, Dan breathed easier. Ester's mount bore down on the campsite, coming in faster now, the big man sitting high in the saddle. Apparently he'd had a glimpse of what had been going on and didn't want to waste time before learning the particulars.

Dan, getting his crutches and standing up, momentarily forgot about his wood-gathering and started back toward camp.

Cabe secured his quirt in the leather-covered clamp on his belt, then came ambling over in Dan's direction.

"What's wrong with you, Dan?" the old-timer asked teasingly. "You go after firewood and don't get any, an' even let a delectable cottontail rabbit get away from you while it was lazin' there almost within arm's reach. An' we both know it would've been extra savory in a stew."

Dan grinned. "Just wasn't thinking, Cabe. But I have a feeling we both became side-tracked there for a while."

Cabe squeezed the young man's shoulder.
"I got your signal, Dan, an' we got out of
the crisis just fine. But for a minute there,
I was sure praying you wouldn't show yourself above that ridge."

Ester reined Galahad to a halt. "It ap-
pears things are still in one piece," he said.
"But who were those two roadrunners who
just left?"

"Members of that Jink Barrett gang,"
Cabe said as Slacker bounded up and gave
his hand a lick. "Jink's shaved his beard,
but that wild-eyed cousin of his sure can't
disguise his looks much. But Dan an' I got
'em bluffed out—nearly, I guess. Then you
made your timely appearance an' they took
off."

"What'd they want?" Ester asked.

"Sizing us up," Cabe said. "Checking over
the place as if they expect to own it sooner
or later. But they weren't sure what they
were up against. I had 'em just about con-
vinced that Dan was in one of the wagons
with a bead on 'em."

"I don't like it," Ester said. "Those gents
are getting a little too bold to suit me."

"You don't have to convince me of that,"
Cabe said. "Bad pennies, that lot, an' you

know what they say about bad pennies."

"Yeah, at some point they'll be back," Ester said, "unless hell freezes over—which
ain't likely in the least."

Chapter 15

One morning, after a night of shooting at Dan Yeager and his friends, Fluke-Eye got up a little late. When he joined the other gang members for breakfast, his cousin, Jink Barrett, and Rim Alum were talking about ending the cat-and-mouse game they'd been playing for the last several days.

Listening for a moment without commenting, Fluke-Eye helped himself to some of Seep Jessup's black coffee.

"There comes a day for direct action," Jink Barrett said, scratching the itchy jawline where his beard had been, "and I think it's about arrived. We can forget the rest."

"You mean you don't think those wagons have anything in 'em worth bothering over?" Rim Alum asked.

"Fluke an' I had our look-see the other day, and even though we didn't get to round out a tally of that ol' gaffer's supply of cans or pounds of pinto beans, I don't think they have anything worth our time."

Jink looked at Fluke-Eye for confirmation.

"About the size of it," the latter agreed.

"Yeah, only a bunch of household goods in that oldster's wagon, an' the smell from that tandem outfit told me we might as well forget it, too. A lot of hide-tanning odors, the only thing I could tell for a certainty— nothing at all to get excited over, Rim, mark my words."

"I hear you," Rim Alum said.

"Might as well settle it with that Yeager," Jink said.

"But it might backfire on you," Rim said. "The Ester gent is as cagey as they come."

"He don't worry us," Fluke-Eye said.

"You two cousins don't have to be in such a hurry, though," Rim Alum suggested. "I might be the newcomer to this outfit, but I've been up an' down this road a lot these last few years, an' I can tell you that big Ester's patterns—which could benefit us if we don't push our luck too soon."

"So you've said," Jink commented dryly.

"It's true, too. For reasons which there's no point in expounding on, I'm not showing

my face again in Boggy Depot. Ah, I had
problems there before I ran into you two.
But when Ester comes this way, he always
stops off there, and he never returns to his
camp empty-handed. So why not play that
angle? We could almost of a certainty add
to our store of trade goods, practically no
doubt about it.

"All I'm saying is, let's give 'em a little
lull once more an' make 'em think they're
free of us, that we've gone off to greener
pastures. Then, after Boggy Depot, when
the timing is just right, give their whole
camp a good lick, pick up the spoils. Or, for
a possible bonus, wait until after Kota, a
little way farther along."

As Jink Barrett pondered the matter, Seep
Jessup put some more wood on his cookfire.
And as he heaped up some hot coals to the
side of his Dutch oven, a faint sputtering
noise was heard.

Seep wasn't much of a talker. But now he
had something to say. "Whatever you gents
decide on, Jink, you'd better be getting me
another Dutch oven soon or you'll be having
to settle for a poor second best in the eating
department. Because this one's cracked, get-

tin' intolerable to cook in. So whenever you make an honest foray someplace, you might give it a thought."

Jink Barrett grinned, his dark eyes crinkling about the corners. "Always griping about something, ain't you, Seep? You're as bad as that old gaffer of Ester's when it comes to the delicate subject of food. I tell you not to fuss, but you insist on hounding me."

"Oh, it's just that I know how partial you are to your vittles, is all, Jink," Seep said as if not wanting to rile the other. "An' this pot here's already way past its judgment day."

"Okay, we'll latch onto something else for you soon, Seep," Jink Barrett said, turning back to Rim Alum. "But right now I'm about at a resolution point, Rim, because every time I think of them Yeagers shooting Bert I get mad all over again." Looking at Fluke-Eye, he added, "I know he was your brother, Fluke, but you're getting all the satisfaction, standing back an' taking potshots at them."

"Oh, I don't mind that at all," Fluke-Eye admitted. "I like to keep 'em guessing, them knowing that sooner or later they'll wake up some morning an' find one less breathing member in their outfit. They're sweatin' it out for sure."

"There's the other point," Rim Alum said patiently.

"But you have no guarantee in it," Jink said with mild reproval. "You claim to know so much, Rim. If you're so smart, why were you so anxious to join up with us, since you already had everything you needed an' then some—according to you?"

"Ah, I had my weak points," Rim Alum said with reluctance. "Put me in a hamlet, why, my vices come to the fore. Drink, for one thing, got me in all sorts of problems. So I knew I had to hit the road for my salvation—luckily runnin' into you gents."

"We took you in, but I reckon I had a weak moment." Jink grinned. "You haven't added one parcel of luck."

"Give me a chance," Rim Alum went on. "As I've said, I know this road, particularly my own section. An' I happen to know this Ester gent an' his sidekick cook have a knife-maker Arkansas friend who has joined their entourage a couple of times that I know of, usually at Boggy Depot or Kota. Seems like the knife-maker always has some kind of business back home while the other two are going back down the trail after another load of something or other. Anyway, they have a tendency to meet in Indian Territory along the road.

"So if you might have in mind to add a cutlery supply to that silverware we found in the barrel when the unfortunate Yeagers had that mishap at that ravine..."

Jink Barrett's wide mouth pulled up at one corner, and he nodded a little.

Rim Alum didn't give the other man a chance to speak before adding, "Expensive handmade cutlery's always in demand, Jink. Even as much as fancy silverware. Wouldn't want you to miss out on something really worthwhile."

"Maybe," Jink said, as if still needing some more thought on the matter.

"Okay, now I've said all my piece," Rim Alum said. "You can make your final decision. But once you let Fluke take his final shot at that Yeager fellow, well, you just might kiss a good-bye to a lot of things. I happen to know this Ester wouldn't sit still long for such an act against his new friend. He'll pull a general halt an' take after you for certain."

"But this young Yeager hasn't been with them long enough to make that kind of difference," Jink said.

"Ester can take up with a person right quick-like, Jink," Rim Alum maintained. "So there you be. If you hit the Yeager youth now, you'll miss out on whatever you might pick up later. Besides, there's one other thing."

"Such as?"

"The last time I happened to see this Arkansas gent, he had along a mighty good-looking young black-haired woman with him. Rumor had it along the road that she was his stepdaughter or other close kinfolk. So you don't know what all you might be missing out on if you strike too soon."

Jink Barrett grinned widely, the red-headed Alum having hit a vulnerable spot. "Well, maybe we'll play 'em along a while longer an' maybe not, Rim. It seems the longer I drag this thing out with the Yeager fellow, the more stale it gets with me, though I'm sure Fluke's giving them something to think about. But I just don't know." He paused. "Black-haired gal, huh?"

Rim Alum nodded. "With all the other necessaries."

"I wonder if she can cook," Jink Barrett mused.

Chapter 16

That same evening, Stormy Ester's entourage made their encampment near Boggy Depot. The night was peaceful enough, but an hour before dawn the next day a spine-tingling squall erupted at the rear of Cabe's wagon.

Reeling awake on his pallet, Dan almost jammed his head against the rear axle of the vehicle, wondering what was going on. He knew that everybody else in camp must have been awakened because the yowl was so loud and so close.

"I sensed your paddin' up here, your highness!" Cabe suddenly said in the semidarkness. "But you can just get the notion outta your head that you can sneak up here any time you want, tryin' to get off with what I've got left of that hog jowl. Git on away from here!"

An animal snarled back at him, clawing at the canvas portion of the wagon as it

119

dropped to the ground. Stunned, Dan looked on speechlessly as he watched the huge cat, weighing perhaps a hundred and fifty pounds, gracefully gliding away.

"Well, thank goodness it didn't scare up the longhorns," Cabe said as he stepped from the Dutch door of his wagon, glancing here and there. "We could've had another stampede with racket like that, huh, Dan?" The oldster, his rifle in his hand, was still peering around. "It did wake you, didn't it?"

"I'll say."

Dan crawled off his pallet as Slacker came up, whining and sniffing at the ground.

"Some watchdog you are," Cabe said. "But you're supposed to be looking after those cattle, ain't you? Besides, that fellow who was here just now could've made mincemeat outta you with one full swipe of its claws."

The dog trotted to the edge of the camp-ground, continuing to sniff the ground.

"Reckon ol' Slacker must have been about as startled for a minute there as I was," Cabe went on. "But I couldn't sleep well for the last hour or so, an' I had a funny feeling that sooner or later we'd have this kind of inspection."

Dan grabbed his crutches beside a wagon

wheel. "Where's Ester?" he asked. "I don't see how he slept through that noise."

"Oh, he got up about a half hour ago an' went to see about Jefferson an' the cattle. Once longhorns stampede as ours have done on a trip like this, they're unpredictable. The least little thing might start them off an' runnin' anew—then again they may doze through a lightnin' storm. We just never know, Dan."

Slacker trotted back, still whining a little. Dan petted the dog's head, asking Cabe, "You've been plagued by big cats along here before, huh?"

"Ozark devil cats," Cabe said, lowering his rifle. "Sometimes they get pesky along this stretch of the road. An' farther along, too. Ah, some folks call 'em panthers, mountain lions, or even cougars. But to me they're just plain ol' Ozark devil cats that C.L. High and I used to have trouble with years ago in Arkansas. Mean, audacious as they can be. Pound for pound, the most vicious foe you could tangle with."

"I'd give 'em a wide berth," Dan said.

"Anybody with a lick of sense would," Cabe agreed. "That one was after that hog jowl I've got hanging there, I suppose. Now

I'll have to fix that rip he or she made in my canvas, too."

"Gave us a good scare," Dan said.

"But just the one like that is really too many, because they most generally have a brother or a sister or some other relative out there in the darkness to back them up. I've got the feeling that the one which came in was only a scout, trying our patience just like that persistent Fire-Shooter."

"I saw a few panthers near San Antonio, but none that large," Dan said.

"An' they get too hungry for their own good," Cabe went on. "That visitor will likely be back, too. Probably not tonight, but soon enough. I've heard of 'em dropping right outta trees on fellows—ripping scalps an' horseflesh at the same time."

"Can you keep 'em scared off?" Dan asked.

"Maybe so, but I don't know how."

Ester rode up on Galahad, catching the end of the conversation. "That noise what I think it was?" he asked Cabe. "I thought maybe this time they'd leave us alone."

"No such luck," Cabe said. "An' you heard right, one of those Ozark devil cats prowling after food."

"I trust it didn't get rewarded."

"Not this time," Cabe said. "I was more'n

half awake an' managed to give it about the same kind of scare it dealt me."

"Well, that's not bad news at all," Ester said. "An' since we're all up, you might as well start breakfast, Cabe."

"Yeah, I know." Cabe stretched and yawned, hoisting his rifle overhead as he did so. Glancing at the sky, he said, "A little later than I thought, for a fact."

Accidentally, the oldster dropped his rifle, and the ensuing shot clanged against the rim of one of Ester's wagon wheels before whining over the resting herd of longhorns.

"An' here we'll probably have some more excitement," Ester prophesied.

He was right.

After a moment of silence, each of the sixty-six longhorns was on its feet and pounding away from the bed-ground.

Dan shook his head. "It sure doesn't take much to get those longhorns on the run, does it?"

"Not really," Ester said with resignation. He clucked to his horse. "Come on, Galahad, we've got some work cut out for us once again."

"Didn't mean to cause it," Cabe said miserably.

"I know," Ester sighed. "But if it's not one

thing, it's something else this trip. We'll be hungry when it's over."

Ester heeled his mount away, Cabe yelping, "I know—that department never changes."

The old-timer shuffled over to the door of his wagon and put his rifle inside very carefully. "Not the best of ways to start off a day," he murmured. "Not good at all, Dan."

The runaway longhorns disrupted the day completely, becoming subdued and allowing themselves to be hazed back to the area of their original bed-ground shortly before sundown.

Ester, Jefferson, and the two trail hands were completely exhausted by this time, and Cabe served them his best son-of-a-gun stew for supper.

"Well, I always like to see ol' Boggy Depot right at the start of a new day, anyway," Ester said, sipping on his third cup of coffee after eating. "So since I didn't make it in today, I'll do it in the morning."

"Hope you're not disappointed," Cabe said. "A lot can happen in a year an' a half's time. She might not even be there. You can't tell."

"Don't try putting any negative notions in my head," Ester countered. "And I want everything here in good shape, too, because I'm showin' off what I've got."

"You don't have to remind me," Cabe said. "I know what to do, since we go through the same ritual every time we get here. So this time let's just hope for decent weather."

"An' this time I don't want your dingy, damp underwear stretched over your wagon tongue when I bring her back here for a look-see," Ester reminded stridently.

"Everything will be spick-and-span," Cabe promised. "While you're gone into town, I'll get everything here in order."

"I trust you will," Ester said, putting his coffee cup down to rub some of the stiffness from the small of his back with his knuckles.

Cabe's two cats came over and he unhooked the rawhide bag from the nail beside the Dutch door of his wagon, dragging it on the ground and playing with the cats a moment as they clawed at the bag, pouncing as if toying with a mouse.

"Yeah, we just might have all kinds of company tomorrow," Cabe mused, "though I do expect C.L. to join us a little later, because first one thing, then another seems to delay him."

"If so, I'll likely run across a letter at the

post office," Ester said.

"Yeah, C.L.'s been pretty good about keeping us posted."

Listening to the pair discussing matters, Dan tested the feel of his broken ankle by lightly bumping his cast against the ground in front of the chair he was sitting on. He decided it felt pretty good even though he knew the bone needed a lot more time to heal.

But it certainly felt good enough to ride into Boggy Depot with Ester—and he was sure the big man wouldn't mind.

Also, Dan figured that his chances of meeting the mysterious Bete were at least fifty-fifty.

Chapter 17

"I'll get busy tonight concocting that favorite chili recipe she's so fond of," Cabe said as he hung up his rawhide bag. "She'll be expecting it, I'm certain."

"I suppose," Ester said. "I plan on having her out here at camp by noon, then back to town before sundown—want her to see what all we have going for us this time."

Cabe said, "She can look an' listen to you all she wants, but you'll never convince her you're about to settle down to one thing, even though you've got such big plans for your harness shop at North Fork Town."

"We'll see about that," Ester said.

Dan continued to be curious about the "she" in their conversation, but he refrained from asking questions. It was as though they were playing a game with him, wanting him to make guesses. But they certainly weren't giving him many clues, and he kept wondering, suspecting he might not get any straight answers if he came right out and asked.

A rainstorm tarried at their campground that night, waking Dan up and threatening to chase him into Cabe's wagon, but he stuck it out, moving his pallet more to the center beneath the vehicle where the rain wasn't blowing. At one point during the downpour, the two cats joined him, Dan barely aware of their presence.

The next morning dawned bright and sunny, and even before Dan could ask his consuming question, Ester himself broached the matter. "You care to ride into Boggy Depot with me after breakfast, Dan? If you want, you could ride your mule, Judy, who's probably getting tired of being tethered behind Cabe's wagon each and every day—or take one of my horses."

"Judy will be fine," Dan said. "We could both use a little variety."

"Good. I've an extra saddle in my wagon, too. One both Cabe an' me had a hand in making back down the road."

They had only a little more than a mile to go, and when they were about halfway there, Dan asked:

"Who's this woman in Boggy Depot that's

so keen on Cabe's chili preparation, Ester?"

"Oh, she's been after Cabe for a couple years now for his chili recipe, but he hasn't given it to her yet, teasing her along and wanting her to guess. But on the subject herself, well, I reckon it wouldn't hurt for you to be in the dark a bit longer, Dan. No earth-shaking matter, though."

Ester chuckled a little, adjusting the chin strap on the new rawhide hat he was still breaking in. "Ah, I figured you might be getting a little curious, though."

As he'd suspected, Dan wasn't going to get a definite answer. "Probably some kinfolk of yours," he said idly.

Ester chuckled some more. "Oh, no— you're not going to pin me down that easy. I've learned that a little curiosity never stunted anybody's growth. And here's something else to think about. Bete and C.L. High just might be there waiting for us, too. So between us we have a lot to look forward to this trip—even though there's a thing or two we'd both like to forget an' be shed of if we had our way."

Dan felt an involuntary tightening of the muscles at the corners of his mouth, knowing Ester had referred to the sniper and the

Jink Barrett gang. He realized how much trouble he was causing Ester and Cabe.

"I appreciate this chance of riding into town here with you, Ester," Dan suddenly said, "but I certainly haven't forgot my main purpose for starting up the Texas Road. An' since I'm causing you and your friends an extra burden—"

It was as far as he got. Ester reined Galahad up and casually took hold of Judy's reins, so he could look Dan in the eye.

"I know what you're thinking, Dan Yeager, and I won't tolerate what you're leading up to. I consider this Fluke-Eye and Jink Barrett as much my problem as they are yours, and you are no longer alone up against them. We'll put our heads together an' deal with 'em in due time, so just bear with me a little, huh?

"An' this is like a holiday we're having today, like a picnic to break up the long push up the road. So we'll just enjoy it—an' no more talk about running out on me, you hear?"

"Well, I didn't—"

"I know, I know," Ester went on, as if still reading Dan's mind. "An' who knows? I might need you to give me a hand once we

get to North Fork Town before you get yourself established in some new venture. We'll
see."

Chapter 18

As they rode into town, Dan noticed Boggy Depot was a thriving community. Several two-story dwellings, businesses, and tree-shaded lawns made the place seem like a picture postcard come to life.

All the stores seemed open for business, and a goodly number of people were in the main street, both Indians and whites. Ester nodded to nearly all of them.

Then at the principal intersection, Ester removed his hat and gave a big wave to an old man sitting in a chair on the porch of a two-story hotel.

"Hello, Zach," Ester said. "I trust business is fine."

The heavyset oldster smiled, peering intently through a pair of spectacles with a clouded lens on the right. "I might not see so well anymore, but I'd recognize that voice any place I heard it. Hello, Ester."

Ester dismounted and shook the man's

hand. "Same ol' trouble, huh?"

"Vision's a little fuzzy, but nothing wrong with my hearing," Zach Rudd proclaimed. "What are you up to?"

"Gonna have that hide and harness shop humming pretty soon at North Fork Town, Zach. Taking a load up there now."

"Just talk," old Zach opined. "You'll just continue making the ruts deeper in the ol' road, back an' forth. Cabe and I both can tell you that."

"We'll see. Ah, Zach, I want you to meet a new friend of mine, Dan Yeager. We're giving him a lift up the road because the Jink Barrett outfit left him stranded, but I won't go into details."

"Pleased to meet you," Dan said.

He started to dismount to shake hands, but Zach shook his head. "No, you just sit tight there, Dan," the oldster said. "I see that you've got a whanged-up ankle, but I can tell from your voice you're not one to sidestep trouble. Welcome to Boggy Depot."

"My pleasure," Dan said.

"Polite, too." Zach nodded. "That's encouraging, what with some of the young pranksters we have around here."

"Kate doing all right?" Ester asked.

"Real fine. An' she's giving this hotel enough competition in the dining endeavors, too. But there's enough traffic for everybody, actually."

"Guess we'd better be getting on up the street to see her."

"Ah, I just happen to know you have a letter at the post office," Zach went on. "Not nosy—just a small town."

"I know—and thanks. We'll drop by there."

Dan swallowed his disappointment, reading between the lines and guessing C.L. High and Bete were not here waiting for them.

"Big Kate will be anxious to see you, Ester. A man couldn't ask for a finer sister," Zach said.

Well, now Dan knew who "she" was.

After remounting, Ester grinned down at the oldster. "So they've started calling her Big Kate, huh?"

"Yeah, an' she got an add-on to that diner of hers since you were here last."

"Such as?"

"Go see for yourself, Ester." Zach nodded a farewell.

A half block up the way they stopped at

the post office and, standing on the porch, Ester read the letter from C.L. High.

"What's the verdict?" Dan heard himself ask.

"They'll meet us at Kota or thereabouts," Ester said.

Dan was disappointed, though he knew it was probably for the best, considering their troubles with the gang.

Presently they both dismounted in front of a huge clapboard building with a sign that said: KATE'S SKILLET.

"There now," Ester said as he secured their mounts' reins to the hitching rail. "Grab your crutches an' let's tromp in here."

Inside, they learned that only about half the available area was devoted to the restaurant business, the rest having been converted into a milliner's shop.

"This is the add-on aspect Zach spoke of," Ester said, pointing to a buxom lady threading a sewing machine. "An' there sits Kate, my little sister who's not so delicate anymore. Being married to a Choctaw Indian must agree with her. Hello, Kate!"

Huge blue eyes blinked at Ester through the doorway, then recognition flooded Kate's rosy-cheeked face. "Stormy!" Smiling, she got up from her chair and rushed to him, hugging her brother with strong arms.

"It seems as if you've been gone forever this time, Stormy!"

He caught her about the waist and swung her around, kissing her solidly on both sides of the face. "You ain't lost a pound," he kidded her. "Matter of fact, you might have put on a few."

"Oh, put me back down," she complained sharply. "You might strain yourself."

"It won't happen," he said. But he put her down anyway, eyeing her critically. "Zach said something about an add-on, but I reckon there's two: your new business here along with the little one you're carrying."

She batted her eyes at him. "Lucky guess," she agreed. "Roy and I expect the new one about Christmas."

"A good present. Is Roy around here today?"

"You've missed him," she said. "He's helping others with some repair work on a bridge back down on the Clear Boggy. He'll be gone a few days."

"Then I won't get to see him at all this time through."

Her chin dropped slightly. "Then you're

not staying here, not settling down after all."

"The last time we were through here I mentioned my harness-shop idea, Kate, remember? Well, it's about to become a reality. I came into town to take you back out to camp so you can have a look-see for yourself at the cattle, my hides, an' everything."

"Oh, I've seen cattle an' hides," Kate said. "You're still daydreaming. But I'm as hungry as a she bear. Hope ol' Cabe has fixed up some good dish as he did the last time."

"He said something about chili," Ester said.

"Sounds like the best," Kate said. "My very favorite, for certain. I can have my rig brought up an' accompany you back." She turned to Dan, smiling brightly. "You work with Stormy?"

"This is Dan Frank Yeager, Kate," Ester said. "He's trailin' along with us as far as we go an' then some."

Noting the crutches and cast, she said, "I trust you're getting along all right, Dan."

"Doing fine," he said. "Ester an' Cabe fixed me up."

"That's good." Turning back to Ester, she asked, "I take it you're heading for North

Fork Town since you're not staying here?"

Ester nodded. "Got me a place all lined up."

"Well, you two go have some coffee or something, Stormy, while I see to my rig."

"Take your time," Ester said. "I need to pick up some flour and a few things."

"Don't buy a ham," she said quickly, "because I'm throwing in one as a gift for your trip. I picked up a bargain on several smoked hams a short while back, and it's perfect for the road."

"Well, okay," Ester said. "Cabe's on the last scrap of his hog jowl, for a fact."

Chapter 19

After obtaining a gunnysack of staples for Cabe's larder, Ester and Dan returned to Kate's front porch just as a man drove up in a shiny buggy pulled by a spirited black horse.

"A horse an' buggy setup like that is a credit to anyone," Ester proclaimed.

Kate strode across the porch, nodding, wearing the most attention-getting hat Dan had ever seen: one fashioned with silk furbelows and flowers.

"I know," she said graciously. "Both horse and buggy were an anniversary gift from Roy."

She held a pink satin parasol ornamented with crystal beads in one hand and a pair of silk gloves in the other, a stark contrast to the rough clothes Dan had noticed so far on this trip.

Ester turned his attention from the buggy to his sister. "You figure you're going to a wedding, Sis? Out there—"

"This is the latest style," she said as she approached her conveyance. "But I suppose you don't see this kind of finery up and down the road, do you?"

"I haven't seen such finery anywhere," Ester admitted, dismounting and moving over to assist Kate into the buggy. "Just don't scare the horses, Sis. Straight from some fancy magazine, huh?"

She nodded. "It's the last word in fashion, Stormy. And I put some back issues of magazines in the buggy a while ago when George here stopped by before circling the block to insure the new harness was properly adjusted."

She introduced her driver, George Green, to the others, adding, "Now we can be off, George. My brother here wants me to go see his traveling circus."

"It represents a new beginning," Ester said.

"That's all well and good." Kate smiled. "Except, of course, for one thing."

"What's that?" Ester asked.

"The harness-shop idea is excellent, Stormy, but you just can't stay put more than a day or so at a time, no matter what you're doing. So I never get my hopes up because I'm awfully familiar with that wandering nature of yours."

By noon they were back in camp, George stopping the buggy a short distance from Cabe's cookfire where the latter was worrying over his chili concoction in the Dutch oven.

"Why, hello, Kate," Cabe said, touching the brim of his hat. "A pleasure to see you once more."

She smiled, twirling her parasol. "I wouldn't have missed this jaunt for anything, Mr. Vesta. And I've brought you some more reading material this time, too."

"That's mighty thoughtful of you, Kate," Cabe acknowledged. "But I still prefer just plain Cabe if you don't mind. An' I want to catch up on my reading, too. Only, on this trip I haven't been able to burn my lamp much on account of—"

"Being so tired an' worn out after a long day's travel," Ester hastened to say.

He gave the oldster a faint headshake, and Dan knew that Ester didn't want Cabe to begin talking about the nocturnal habits of the bothersome Fire-Shooter.

"Yeah, that's a fact," Cabe went on, getting the cue. "We've been racking up good mileage about every day—leaving little time for much else."

"Well, you'll have the extra magazines along in case you do get the chance to continue your reading," Kate said, accepting George's hand to step down from the buggy. "And the spicy aroma in the air here tells me I'm in for a treat."

The remark brought forth an appreciative grin. "One of the best chili dinners comin' up that you'd ever hope to run across in a month of Sundays, Kate."

She nodded with enthusiasm. "Nobody can make chili as good as yours, Cabe. I appreciate fine chili and so do my customers back at my restaurant. And *this* time, I'm confident you're going to share that secret ingredient I've never been able to identify."

Cabe shook his head with a snap. "Ah, sorry, Kate, but you know how some of us cooks are—some things here an' there we just can't seem to part with. If I told you right out, it would only spoil the challenge of guessing for you."

"I could survive if you dropped the hint," Kate sighed, knowing she was going to lose out to the oldster's stubbornness once again.

"Experiment some," Cabe said vaguely.

"I have, but I'll never come up with what's missing in it. I've tried about every possible condiment I can think of, too. So are you sure you won't—"

Cabe seemed to hesitate for an instant, then firmly shook his head. "Not this trip, Kate. It wouldn't be fair to you. But just think: today you're getting another opportunity to see if you can identify what you haven't scared up."

"Well, I'll have to warn you, I'm all ready this time, Cabe Vesta. I haven't eaten today, and my taste buds are extra honed, maybe on the edge of discovery."

"That's mighty fine," Cabe said. "You may even return to town with increased savvy in the culinary arts. I certainly respect confidence like yours. Though, as I've indicated, I wouldn't dream of curbing your creative speculations."

"Fancy talk for stubbornness is all I'm hearing, *Mr.* Cabe Vesta. But, regardless, I'm ready to try some of your specialty, even though I'll probably go back to my restaurant knowing no more than I do this minute."

"We'll just see about that," Cabe said, still seemingly offering her a bit of hope.

Raising the lid on his Dutch oven, Cabe dipped his wooden ladle into the chili mixture and sniffed at the results. He nodded, smiling widely at his admirer.

"It's ready, Kate."

"Well, I am, too."

"Be just as you remembered it."

"I can tell if it is or not," Kate assured him.

"I've the utmost confidence in your abilities, Kate. I'll get those wooden bowls I steam-cleaned this morning. Somehow the wooden bowls seem to add to the flavor, I've found."

"That's a moot point, but I'll go along with it," Kate said. "Now do you really prefer to serve it with crackers or bread?"

"Mainly, I serve it to eat," Cabe joked. "But I have both biscuits and some crackers now that Ester picked up my supplies, so, actually, it's a matter of personal preference."

Moments later, after everyone had sampled the steaming bowls of chili, Kate agreed that it was indeed delicious, fit for the most discriminating of palates. Still, the overall meal was not a galloping success because it commenced raining, the deluge hitting so rapidly that the wooden bowls of chili were abruptly diluted with rainwater, ruining Cabe's effort—except for what was later salvaged from the covered Dutch oven.

But for the moment, everyone's primary concern was to seek shelter. And the rain wouldn't let up, either, the upshot being that Kate and her driver couldn't immediately return to Boggy Depot, having to bed down in Ester's camp. Ester made room for his sister in his own wagon while the menfolk crowded up in Cabe's, sleeping very listlessly.

Miraculously, soon after midnight, the clouds drifted northward and the sky became clear. Moonlight bathed the countryside, and all was quiet—until a short time before sunup.

Chapter 20

The first shot hit the coffeepot next to the chili-laden Dutch oven Cabe had abandoned in the rain hours before. Dan was awake with a start, clambering off his pallet in Cabe's crowded wagon, banging his head against one end of the cot, where Kate's driver, George, was lying.

Ester, who'd been dozing in a chair near the cot, almost toppled to the floor as he awoke. And Cabe, who had a narrow bed built into the front part of the wagon, got to one elbow immediately, offering advice.

"Don't jump into the open where you might get shot!" he said. Then, raising his voice, he added, "Kate, you stay put in Ester's wagon an' don't you dare get up! Seems some danged fool out there must have overshot a rabbit or something!"

"I hear you, Cabe," she called back. "You don't have any idea who it might be?"

"No," Cabe lied. "So keep down—he might take another shot or two."

"Yeah, no point in getting Sis worked up over this," Ester said, going along with Cabe's approach. "I'll just be glad to get her back into town."

"Then this is not the first time it's happened?" George asked, sitting up on the cot and peering at Ester in the dimness.

"No, it's not," Ester stated without embellishment. "And don't you dare let Sis know of this, George. No point in having her worried about it—understand?"

"Why, sure, but—"

"Better lie back down, George," Ester advised. "You'll have a little more protection that way."

George was already in a prone position before Ester finished the recommendation. And within seconds a zinging whine broke the quiet at the rear of the wagon.

"Just flirtin' with us," Cabe said.

"Once more should do it this time," Dan predicted. "It'll be good and light before long, and he'll be making some tracks away from here."

"Speaking of which, I'll saunter out his

way and have a look-see this morning," Ester said. "What with that rain, he'll be leaving some good tracks for me."

"Ester, that man out there is still shooting," Kate pointed out in a muted, uneasy voice from the other wagon. "Shouldn't you let him know he's getting too close to us?"

"Yeah, you're right, Sis."

Dan saw the big man shrug a shoulder in the faint light that was now entering Cabe's wagon.

To the menfolk, Ester said, "I guess I'll play along—I really don't think it'd hurt much of anything. However, Dan, we're both getting fed up with these potshots, aren't we?"

So saying, Ester crawled to the rear of the wagon and, quickly poking his head outside, shouted: "Try another direction, mister! You'll get nothing but trouble shootin' this way!"

It worked—for about five full seconds. Then another shot followed.

"Better tell him again, Ester," Kate suggested. "I need to get an early start back to town, and George and I can't leave here with such shooting going on."

"I know, Sis," Ester acknowledged. "Let's just give him a minute now—he must have heard me."

This time there was no repeat performance, the Fire-Shooter sticking to his three-shot pattern, knowing that full daylight would presently be against him.

"There, that's what I've been waiting for," Ester said. "That gent will be leaving about now, and I'll go see if I can cut his sign."

"I was a gunsmith formerly," George volunteered, "an' those shots sounded as if they might have come from the muzzle of an old Sharps carbine. Some of those old Navy models I worked on were mighty accurate, too. I've a feelin' that fellow out there is awfully sure of himself."

Presently Ester took his saunter into the area where the Fire-Shooter had been, but he didn't make his report until Kate and her driver were on their way back to Boggy Depot after breakfast.

Reaching in a pocket, Ester brought forth a cartridge, which he claimed had still been warm when he picked it up. "So George was right about the caliber," Ester said, holding up the empty case for Cabe and Dan to see. "This is a .36, the official Navy bore."

"Well, I didn't want to burden George with too much information, because I didn't know what he might let slip to Kate," Cabe said, "but it was an old Navy carbine that this Fluke-Eye was holding across his lap when he and his cousin, Jink, visited our camp."

"Well, my fuse is getting a little short where that bunch is concerned," Ester said. "An' I've a hunch our trails will be crossing again soon."

Chapter 21

At last the sixty-six cattle were delivered in Falcon City. Allen Jefferson and his two hands departed then. But Cabe and Ester and Dan continued to head north.

A few miles from the settlement of Kota two evenings later, C.L. High drove his wagon and two horses into their camp. Stepping down from his seat, he held out a hand to Ester. As the pair shook, Dan noted at least half a dozen knife handles protruding from the inside of the tall man's coat.

"I see you're still as well armed as ever," Ester said, also noticing.

"I know it," C.L. said, nodding at Cabe and looking at Dan. "Who's your friend here?"

"Dan Frank Yeager," Ester said.

"Glad to know you," Dan said, easing forward on his crutches and shaking the man's hand.

Then immediately he turned to the young

lady stepping down from the other side of the wagon. "Let me assist you," Dan said, careful not to trip over himself with the crutches as he did so.

Cabe was right, he thought. She had the blackest eyes he'd ever seen, and he felt drawn to her like a pin to a magnet.

She smiled at him, and he felt a warmth spread in his chest.

"Why, I do believe we have a gentleman here," she said with a hint of boldness, accepting Dan's hand. "Good-looking, too."

"My stepdaughter, Bete," C.L. said. "Needless to say, she's not the least bit shy, and I've not been able to keep track of all the suitors she's turned down—eyes set on the impossible, I guess. Hadn't been for her things, I wouldn't have needed that extra horseflesh to get us here."

Cabe, about to exit his own wagon, said, "Sounds as if that's your cookstove in there, Bete."

"It is," she said. "I'd intended to get my special man with the use of that. But maybe..." She looked at Dan closely.

"Maybe what?" Ester prompted.

"Maybe I've found him," she said, lightly

touching Dan's arm. "You always have to use those crutches?"

"No," Dan said, feeling as if he were in a half daze. "Just a broken ankle."

"First rawhide cast I've ever seen," Bete said.

"Me, too," Dan informed her. "It's coming off soon."

C.L. High, observing the pair, nodded knowingly. "Well, she's had me haul that stove around for some time now, but I've had a feelin' she'd light up sooner or later without having to strike a match."

"It could happen like that," Ester agreed. "Bete, you're prettier each time I see you. I don't know why you can't see your way to falling for me."

"You're too much like kinfolk, Stormy," Bete said, unable to take her dark gaze from Dan. "I think I can rest that stove now."

Dan didn't know exactly what comment to make and automatically blurted, "But I don't care if you can cook or not."

"I can manage," Bete said. "You been on the road long, Dan?"

Dan grinned. "Just about long enough, I think."

Ester and C.L. exchanged glances.

C.L. said, "Climate been okay this trip?"

"Can't complain. How was your trip this fine month of June?"

"My, I suppose it is June already, isn't it?" C.L. said, sounding mildly astounded. "Time sure flits away."

"You don't take time to notice much of anything unless it has to do with your cutlery work," Bete said pointedly.

C.L. pulled himself up to his full height, which came to well over six feet. "Now, Bete, I wouldn't say that."

"But it's true," Bete said, gentle reproval in her voice. "We're both well aware of that."

"Yeah, well, to answer your question, Ester, we had a safe, overburdened, uneventful trip, thank you."

"Anybody hungry?" Cabe interjected.

"All of us, I'll wager," C.L. said confidently.

Dan had his thoughts on other things. Watching for Bete's reaction, he said, "I've never heard of a stove being put to that use," just to see if she would elaborate.

She looked him straight in the eye, and he was barely aware of the few tiny freckles on the bridge of her nose.

"I don't think I'll be needing the ruse any-more, Dan. But it was a good idea, though, don't you think?"

"I don't think you would have needed it at all," Dan said.

"You work for Ester and Cabe?"

"No—I'm just their lucky passenger, it seems."

"Destination?" she asked.

"Fort Gibson. You been there?"

"Yes," Bete said. "Jake Lamont's the sut-ler there, and he also happens to be my grandfather."

Dan was pleasantly surprised. "I have business with your Grandfather Lamont." He didn't continue, for the last thing he wanted to do was alarm her about their po-tential danger.

"This certainly is an amazing coinci-dence," she said, batting her eyes at him. "We...we'll see how everything turns out, won't we?"

"It's one thing I'm not planning to miss," Dan said, wishing he could kick his cast off.

Cabe addressed C.L. High. "You ready to go to work with those knives you're so handy with? We've got plenty of leather to start with when we hit North Fork Town."

At the mention of his favorite subject, C.L.'s face brightened considerably. The work coat he was wearing had an extra long tail, and he spread it open, revealing knife handles poking from at least two dozen sheaths sewn into the lining of the garment, almost from knee to shoulder.

"If anybody needs a knife, he can check in with me," he said, grinning. "I'll even fix up something special, if required. I've got all the proper equipment for any job right here in the wagon, Cabe, makeshift forge an' all."

"I believe you, C.L. Sounds like I'm listening to an authority on the subject."

"You are," C.L. said without diffidence. "I suppose you've made up some of your road-brand chili this trip?"

Cabe nodded. "For another meal. But I saved most of it, planning on serving it tonight."

"Well, that sounds fine. You season it up just right. Thinking about it makes my mouth water. I must be awfully hungry without knowing it."

"Well, I'll have that traveler's delight ready in no time at all," Cabe said. "Probably a big day coming up tomorrow."

* * *

In the middle of the night, when everyone was asleep, the panther returned. And this time it brought a friend along, each as hungry as could be, lured by the pungent odor of the smoked ham Cabe had hung inside his wagon near the Dutch door.

The larger of the big cats got on the wagon steps and thrust its head and shoulders above the closed lower part of the door. Lunging half inside the wagon, it grasped the ham with its huge teeth and yanked, breaking the twine suspending the prize from the wagon top.

Then, as soon as it bounded back outside, its partner decided not to delay getting its share of the meat, and the whole camp was awakened by the marauders as they leaped across the campground, each one of them trying to demolish most of the ham.

Before anyone could react effectively to the panthers, three plundering horsemen thundered up from the south edge of camp to execute a kidnapping planned by their leader, who'd recently become impatient with Seep Jessup's cooking and who'd also decided he needed some female company.

Rim Alum   was quickly dismounting and

scooping up Cabe's handy Dutch oven. And Fluke-Eye, as if acting on impulse, reached out in the moonlight and plucked Cabe's rawhide bag from the rear of the wagon. A lot of the bag's contents got spilled over Dan's rawhide cast as he rested on his pallet beneath Cabe's wagon. Everything was happening so fast, Dan hardly knew what was what.

Bete was sleeping in the rear of C.L. High's wagon, her head toward the tailgate. Jink Barrett already knew where she was—thanks to Fluke-Eye's efforts earlier with his telescope—and he hastily dismounted. Keeping a rein in his hand, he quickly pulled her out of the wagon. Dazing her with a rap to the jaw, he loaded her over his saddle and then leaped up behind her, ruthlessly heeling his horse away.

Dan, watching through the spokes of a wagon wheel, was stunned. But only for an instant. Then he rolled out from under the wagon, grabbing his crutches and knowing he must mount Judy and give chase.

Chapter 22

"They've got Bete!" Dan yelped as he hobbled toward his staked-out mule. "The Jink Barrett outfit!"

Two shots burned the air as the gunmen charged away, but no one was hurt.

C.L. High was too upset to do anything useful just then.

Meanwhile, Ester stumbled from his lead wagon, struggling with his pants. "You say they've got Bete?"

"Jink Barrett and his friends!" Dan called. "I'm going after 'em!"

Ester buckled his belt as the details sank in. For a couple of seconds he watched Dan trying to bridle the mule, the crutches hampering him.

Ester rushed forward to help, but by then a determined Dan was already swinging aboard the mule, dropping his crutches as he did so.

"You sure you're up to this, Dan?" the big man asked.

"Yes—I'm going."

"Then take this." Ester handed Dan a revolver. "I see you've got your Green River
knife there in your belt sheath, so this should
complete your hardware in case you need
it. I cleaned an' loaded it last night, a companion to my own Colt. I'll get Galahad an'
be right with you, Dan. Now don't—"

Dan didn't wait for Ester to finish. He was
rushing off in the direction the desperadoes
had taken.

Racing along, the young rider had a fleet-
ing thought about the two panthers who had
initially awakened him. And almost at once
Dan had a moonlit glimpse of the two big
cats, somewhere ahead of him, fighting for
the ham.

Dan never did know how it happened, but
during the cats' struggle, the ham abruptly
tumbled free and bounced into some blackberry bushes. And Judy, Dan's mule, already heading for almost the same spot, hit
them sideways in such a manner that the
ham landed on Dan's midriff with a solid
thump.

Reacting automatically, Dan grasped the
ham with his free hand as Judy regained
her stride. He continued riding in the direction the Barrett outfit had taken, plan-

ning to toss the ham down—to keep the two panthers busy for a while.

But before Dan could get rid of the meat, his attention was diverted by Ester's voice drifting through the brush: "Dan's following 'em, Cabe, an' I'm on my way! We've got to get Bete!"

Then the next thing Dan knew, he heard a muffled thumping sound as Galahad and Ester hit the ground.

There was a discouraging shout from Ester: "Galahad, you shouldn't stumble over roots like that—now we'll both need help getting up!"

Dan didn't slow down, knowing both Cabe and C.L. High were within hearing distance of the big man's voice. He also realized that now he was alone rushing after the enemy, but he'd never felt so determined about anything in his life.

Without thinking, Dan continued to hug the ham to his chest. Above him, the sky showed its anger with clouds and lightning, with no rain following. Judy pranced sideways, fright surging through her bloodstream. Dan nearly fell out of the saddle. Yet somehow he managed to keep his balance—and the ham.

"Easy, Judy," he soothed. "Easy now."

The mule seemed to calm down for a moment, but soon the sky became angrier than ever, with more lightning—and thunder, too.

Ahead of Dan, the gunmen were cursing the stormy display. Then a fresh bolt of lightning spooked Judy, causing her to run madly for a fair distance.

Then she stopped abruptly, exhausted, and decided to lie down. Dan was barely able to keep from getting trapped beneath her.

He shouldered his way into the ground hard, managing not to bang his broken ankle against anything. The ham was now near his head—and the panthers were running toward him.

Chapter 23

The panthers had almost reached Dan when he finally tossed the ham toward them, hoping they would forget about him.

It worked. Both cats were pouncing on the meat almost at once. One grabbed it between its strong jaws, and then both of them were heading in the same direction as the Barrett gang.

For a few heartbeats Dan lay perfectly motionless. Meanwhile, Judy came back to life and tried to stand up.

Elated that his mule wasn't as fagged out as he'd thought, Dan hobbled over and grabbed the reins.

"Don't rush it, Judy," he cautioned.

But by now the mule was on all fours, snorting and looking around wildly. Dan petted the animal as cloud masses overhead separated and moved away, letting shafts of moonlight skip over the land. The panthers had settled their differences, it seemed, and from the northwest, Dan caught the sound of voices.

Not wanting to let the Barrett outfit get too far away, he felt around on the ground for a suitable support stick to take the place of his crutches. Finding one, he started moving again, for the present leading Judy.

To Dan's great surprise, one of the panthers sprang at Judy from the side, and its partner could be heard nearby. Dan was terrified, but the sturdy mule somehow frightened both cats off in no time.

Quickly mounting Judy, Dan started in the direction he'd heard the voices.

He had not gone far when he distinctly heard the click of a weapon's hammer being drawn back—then came a scratchy sound as one of the panthers sprang from a tree, claws spread, toward the dark form with the gun.

BAM!

A cluster of shotgun pellets knocked Dan's hat from his head as he rolled sideways from the mule, spilling to the ground as Judy bolted away, tangling one of the reins around his left wrist. Dan managed to hang onto his transportation, but the man with the shotgun wasn't as lucky: the poised panther, frightened by the weapon's blast, was clawing viciously at the assailant.

The man's hat skittered off his head when long, sharp claws ripped across his scalp, tearing and digging in cruelly.

"Help!" the man screamed.

His finger automatically clamped down on the second trigger of his double-barreled shotgun, the pellets striking the panther in its underside, doing massive damage, knocking the animal to the ground.

Dan held onto the rein wrapped around his wrist, twisting it tighter, not wanting Judy to get away. The mule finally stopped, and Dan secured the reins to a stumpy tree, then moved cautiously over to the downed man.

The moon lit up the victim's face, a streak of blood running down one cheek. His eyes stared vacantly upward, as if he were dead.

Dan knew this man was not Jink Barrett himself, nor was it Fluke-Eye. Knowing he couldn't tarry, Dan picked up the shotgun to substitute for his crutches now and, nudging the cat to insure it was dead, he hobbled back to Judy and mounted up. Judy was ready to get away from there, striking a trot along a wide trail.

Ten minutes later, Dan grew wary as he approached a section of the trail where everything suddenly seemed strangely frozen, strangely quiet. But the stillness lasted only until the second panther sprang at a man standing among some trees just as the latter fired a rifle, creasing Dan's right temple, tossing him off Judy onto the ground with numbing impact. Dan grunted and turned, coming up with the Green River knife in his right hand, Ester's Colt having flipped from his waistband.

Dan saw the man with the rifle attempt to defend himself—but the fellow didn't have a chance against the big cat. The heavy panther pushed the man to the ground, then began to claw at his face.

Groaning, the man lost hold of his rifle, which toppled against the flank of the big cat. But the panther paid no attention to the gun at all, knowing there'd be no more trouble from the downed man.

Instead, the cat moved toward Dan.

Judy bolted and tried to get away, but a hoof became caught among some roots, tripping the mule, slamming it to the earth as Dan rolled free. On his back now, Dan wrenched his body, getting his elbows beneath him.

He gripped the Green River knife in his
hand, but the weapon seemed as heavy as
an anvil.

Chapter 24

The huge cat paused for a second and Dan became stone still. Moving toward him now, the panther bent down to Dan's broken ankle, gnawing a little on the rawhide cast.

When Dan felt the sharp teeth scratch against his skin, he came alive with a jolt.

In one motion, he lurched forward and sliced at the panther with his sharp knife.

Luckily, this was enough. The wild feline leaped up, abruptly startled, and bounded swiftly toward safer country.

Catching his breath, Dan crawled and half dragged himself over to Judy, the animal still down and fighting the root entanglement. It was all Dan could do to get the captive hoof free without being knocked down himself.

"You're okay, Judy," he said. "Calm down."

Getting upright, Judy shook herself, as if to get rid of her trailside troubles, but Dan knew the worst might yet come.

Holding onto a rein, Dan tied it to a sapling and, after finding the shotgun for support, went over to the man sprawled on the ground. There was no movement at all in the fellow, and a death stare kept his eyes gazing blankly—with one eye angling away from the nose.

"Fluke-Eye," Dan gasped.

Leaning over, he picked up the man's rifle and examined it. It was the .36 weapon, all right. The Fire-Shooter's gun.

But where was Jink Barrett himself? And, more important, where was Bete? What had become of them?

After retrieving Ester's Colt revolver, Dan mounted Judy and cautiously rode on, keeping to the wide trail.

About fifteen minutes later they approached a stretch of road leading to a dark stand of low-limbed trees and having what appeared to be huge boulders on either side. And as Dan was thinking about what an ideal place it would be for an ambush, Judy's ears lifted suddenly, pointing forward. Then the mule balked, refusing to take another step.

Dan gave up trying to force the animal onward, sensing that he might be better off on his own. So he dismounted and, continuing with the shotgun as a support in walking, started after his prey alone, staying in the deepest shadows, putting a little weight now and then on the cast, hoping the makeshift protector would hold up under the stress.

His every sense alert, Dan imagined that danger lurked behind every bush, and he strained his eyes so as not to miss any telltale movement of his enemy. Pausing after a moment, he listened intently as he rested against the trunk of an elm tree, gradually identifying the sound of running water. Ordinarily, the sound of water would be reassuring, but as Dan resumed his stalking, he reminded himself that in all likelihood he was *not* the only person hearing it.

Again he stopped, his nostrils widening, detecting the aroma of someone's cooking: he was nearing a campsite of some sort. An ideal location for parties preying on travelers on the Texas Road.

Yes, Dan thought, he must have followed Jink Barrett to his current lair.

Splotches of moonlight appeared around him, and Dan backed into the shadow of a tree. Looking ahead carefully, he was positive the huge rounded mounds were indeed boulders, and on one of them he saw what appeared to be a silhouette of a big panther—or were his eyes playing tricks on him?

Then he noticed a faint movement in the semidarkness ahead. His right hand gripped the butt of the Colt Ester had lent him. But Dan's enemy fired at him first. Both men shot several times—and finally Dan blacked out.

Dan had no awareness of time—but it was full daylight when he came around to join the living, Cabe hovering over him, dabbing a damp cloth to his forehead.

"You'll be as good as new soon now," the oldster opined as Dan blinked his eyes. "You haven't been hurt—just stunned."

"What's that?" Dan asked, his sight still blurry from his black, silent world. He thought the boulder in his direct line of vision supported a poised, angry panther. But as his sight cleared, he saw that the object was only a dead cedar stump protruding from the other side of the boulder.

"Ah, thank goodness," Dan mumbled, feeling silly.

"Good to have you awake, young man," Cabe said. "An' you may give yourself a pat on the back, because you flat out single-handedly wiped out the biggest part of the Jink Barrett gang!"

"I had some help."

"Yeah, I noticed you did," Cabe said, "since I've been trailing you. Sometimes those devil cats are awfully unpredictable, an' their trying to satisfy their own wants played right into your hands, this time. But I'll just stick with Thorny an' Mesquite, myself."

"Don't blame you there."

"Well, Jink Barrett, the big-shot gunman, is lying right over yonder," Cabe said, indicating a blanketed form nearby. "An' you probably realize that one of those other fellows back down the road is what's left of Fluke-Eye."

"Yeah, I know," Dan said. "What about the other man, Cabe—the first one who got killed? The one with the shotgun?"

"A bit of a coincidence there, Dan," Cabe went on. "Jefferson once explained to me that he was a man out of his past of about three years ago—name of Rim Alum. Jefferson an' this Alum had some misunderstanding. Jefferson didn't elaborate. But it led to a shootout during which Jefferson got shot in the hand and ultimately lost it, due to infection, having to switch over to that iron knob he has now. But he's learned to live with it."

"Were there just the three members left of the Jink Barrett outfit?" Dan asked.

"No, there was—still *is,* actually—a fourth member, but he has always been no more than a flunky for the others." Cabe paused, gesturing in the direction of the rippling water nearby. "There he is, comin' along with Ester now. Name's Seep Jessup, an' he was the one needing that Dutch oven of mine that Rim Alum had tied to his saddle."

Dan turned his head and gazed in the direction Cabe was indicating, seeing the nondescript man with a floppy-brimmed hat strolling up with Ester.

Scowling worriedly, Dan asked, "Where's Bete?"

Cabe blinked, obviously not knowing. "Why, I just about got here myself, Dan," the oldster said. "We'll have to ask Ester an' see if he might know something."

Chapter 25

When Ester and Seep Jessup came over, Dan repeated his question. "Where's Bete?"

Ester grinned, thumbing back his rawhide hat. "Thought you might be interested in that department, Dan. She's all right, back there in the Barrett camp trying to get your barrel of silverwear straightened out. It seems that the troublemakers had been using some of it, but they didn't do any damage."

An hour later everybody was back in Ester's camp, getting ready to continue the journey. Of necessity, the bodies had been disposed of in crevices along the boulders where plenty of rocks were handy, Seep Jessup doing most of the work. The silver barrel had been transferred from the plunder wagon to C.L. High's wagon because it had the most room to spare.

Ester sent the last member of Barrett's gang away, saying, "Next time, Mr. Jessup,

I suggest you be more careful in choosing your associates. Otherwise, you might not get off so light. You understand?"

Jessup swallowed. "You bet I do, mister. I get your drift with no problem. An' I hope I can do a little better."

"I solemnly hope so," Ester said.

Touching his hat respectfully, the old man clucked to his Spanish mules and headed south on the Texas Road.

"You're too merciful," Cabe chided.

"Intuition." Ester grinned. "Jessup was kept knuckled under by those others. Now that he's on his own, though, I believe he'll have a fair chance to straighten out."

Cabe's two cats, Thorny and Mesquite, came up to the chair where Dan was sitting, resting his broken ankle on a stump. Springing onto the stump, they both began nuzzling against the cast, purring with gusto.

"You like that rawhide smell?" Dan asked. "Good, huh?"

Absently, Cabe unhooked his rawhide bag from the nail on his wagon and, about to use it in playing with the cats as was his wont, he suddenly stopped, looking at Dan and chuckling. "It's not the rawhide itself,

Dan," he explained. "Remember how that Ozark devil cat you mentioned was so attracted to your cast last night? Well, Thorny an' Mesquite are putting on the same kind of act for you. Only, they're not trying to take so big a bite."

"What does it mean?"

Cabe opened the leather bag and took out a pinch of its contents. He sprinkled the crushed leaves and flower petals in the grass at the edge of the stump, and the two cats promptly began wallowing around near the stuff, purring with even more determination.

Dan grinned. "I know what that must be," he said.

"You're probably right, Dan. When the Barrett outfit hit us, Fluke-Eye grabbed the rawhide bag on the run, just to be stealing something, I guess, an' I was lucky to find it later. But when he made off with it, the material tore some, and a little of the 'condiments' must have spilled over your broken ankle. So, since these cats went into a tizzy over it—"

"Catnip in that bag, huh?" Dan said.

"For a fact," Cabe said.

C.L. High stepped over, his nose twitching. He hadn't heard their conversation, but he smiled with a flash of enlightenment. "That odor," he mused, "is somehow mighty familiar—connected with last night's supper, I do believe."

"Ah, congratulations," Cabe said. "Catnip."

C.L. High straightened up to his full height and glared down his nose at Cabe. "I particularly associate it with my bowl of *chili*. You are not supposed to put something like that in *our* food!"

Cabe's mouth dropped. "Well, I—"

Ester came up and so did Bete, who had gone into C.L. High's wagon to change into a fresh dress.

"What's this about catnip in the chili?" Ester wanted to know.

Cabe looked sheepish, then smiled confidently, as if thinking he could talk his way out of his dilemma. "No great harm done, Ester," the oldster said. "Ah, you know how well your sister, Kate, likes my chili an' how she's tried to wheedle me out of that 'special' ingredient I put in it?"

"Yeah," Ester said dubiously.

"Well, the very first time Kate tried my chili, I'd accidentally spilled a little catnip in it, an' I just didn't mention it to anybody. Then, when she raved on so much about it, well, I didn't have the heart to tell her what the 'secret' condiment was I was using. So I just dropped the matter there an' then.

"But now every time I know Kate's going to have some more of my chili, I've made sure to put in a little catnip so she won't be disappointed. You can't blame me, can you?"

Ester was shaking his head, obviously sharing C.L.'s misgivings. "Well, I happen not to be a cat," he said. "So from now on out, I'll thank you to just skip your special ingredient, huh?"

Cabe shrugged a shoulder. "Well, if that's the way you feel about it."

"I do."

"So be it then," Cabe said piously—but the twinkle in his eyes didn't quite match what he was promising.

Turning to Dan, Ester put a heavy hand on his shoulder. "The ankle okay after your ordeal?" he asked.

"Coming along fine."

"Good." Ester rocked back on his heels, as if sizing Dan up anew. "Want to do me a favor?"

"Of course."

"I'm going to need a good, steady man at the North Fork Town harness shop, Dan. And if you could help out, we might even start up a little silversmith business on the side, since you already know as much as you do about it. Besides, I'll likely be on the road quite a bit."

Here Ester gave Cabe a sidelong glance, then quickly turned back to Dan. "What do you say?"

Dan was already nodding, his chest tight. And he was thinking that both Cabe and Ester's sister, Kate, were right: the big man didn't intend to settle down. The Texas Road was his home, he wasn't about to abandon it for any steady business in town.

"I know you'll want to get that silverware and stuff on up to the sutler at Fort Gibson, Dan," Ester went on. "A few sets might be missing, but I know you'll be able to settle all that with the sutler. Bete's grandfather should be a reasonable man, even though I've never met the gent."

Bete moved closer to Dan, her black eyes moist and bright as she looked at him. Then she gave him a hug and kissed him on the lips. "I saw in your eyes you were wanting to do that, Dan, so I thought it wouldn't be unladylike to help you out, under the circumstances. But from now on, you'll have to earn such endearments."

"I'm the best worker you'll ever have around, Bete," Dan promised, his heart flooded with his love for her.

Ester glared at Bete. "You real positive who you want to use that cookstove for, Bete? There's still time to reconsider."

She shook her head with firmness. "Ester, you'll always be too much like family to me."

"Yeah, I know," Ester said. "You're kinda like a sister to me, too." He then glanced at Dan. "I hope you realize how fortunate your luck is running, Dan."

"Indeed I do, Stormy," Dan said. He turned to Bete. "It's like the beginning of a journey all over again, even though I'm more than halfway there. And I'm in no hurry to get to the end of the trip, considering the recent changes."

Bete smiled at Dan, reaching for his hand as she did so. Dan found her touch warm and promising.